THE TOUCHSTONE

EDITH WHARTON

THE TOUCHSTONE

Preface and Epilogue by Cynthia Griffin Wolff

HarperPerennial
A Division of HarperCollinsPublishers

Originally published by Charles Scribner's Sons in 1900.

THE TOUCHSTONE. Preface, Epilogue, and Selected Bibliography copyright ©
1991 by Cynthia Griffin Wolff. All rights reserved. Printed in the United States
of America. No part of this book may be used or reproduced in any manner
whatsoever without written permission except in the case of brief quotations
embodied in critical articles and reviews. For information address HarperCollins
Publishers, 10 East 53rd Street, New York, NY 10022.

First HarperPerennial edition published 1991.

Library of Congress Cataloging-in-Publication Data

Wharton, Edith, 1862–1937.
    The touchstone / by Edith Wharton: preface by Cynthia Griffin
Wolff.—1st HarperPerennial ed.
        p.   cm.
    Includes bibliographical references.
    ISBN 0-06-097379-X (pbk.)
    I. Title.
PS3545.H16T68   1991   90-55808
813'.52—dc20

91 92 93 94 95 CC/MPC 10 9 8 7 6 5 4 3 2 1

Preface

*I*t is a remarkable fact that although a great many men have begun their novel-writing careers with fictional accounts of their youthful apprenticeship, until recently, most major women novelists have never written fictional accounts of their apprenticeship at all. In their *Künstlerromane* (their stories of the struggle to become an author), men have traditionally recounted a variety of hardships: the painful childhood of a preternaturally sensitive boy; an adolescence tormented by conflict—between passionate sexual desire and the need to forswear the flesh for the higher demands of vocation, between the mundane demands of family and friends who think in terms of business or trade and the demands of a purely aesthetic life—and a young adulthood during which success may tempt the artist into satisfying the inferior judgment of a tasteless marketplace. Throughout, there are certain unending themes: the loneliness of the vocation; the relentless self-discipline that is required to perfect a work; the disheart-enment and self-doubt that must often be conquered. In each case the particulars of the story are different. How-ever, the protagonist's talent, his uniqueness, his "right" to feel in some measure "misunderstood" is an unques-tioned presupposition of *all* such fiction.

By contrast, female artists have traditionally adopted a variety of defensive postures that seem designed primar-ily to deny and obscure the uncertainty, conflict, and pain of their personal development. Furthermore, although this attitude is easiest to observe in major women authors (because it is reflected in their written work), it has by no means been limited to them. Patricia Meyer Spacks has published a study of women's autobiographical work that is suggestively entitled "Selves in Hiding" and that exam-ines the autobiographical writing of distinguished public women such as Emma Goldman and Golda Meir. What Spacks reveals is a consistent lack of realistic self-appraisal in these women's assessment of their own achievements—a manner that protests, "What I did was not particularly unusual, not fundamentally different from what *anyone* might have done in my place. I am not special; probably, I am really not worth noticing." Thus in the accounts of their own lives, these women reported their public accom-plishments with such matter-of-fact diffidence that personal disclosure was effectively excluded.

Far from being unique, then, the profound reticence of women novelists actually reveals a hesitation that afflicts a great many successful women—the result of some humil-iating pain, perhaps, or the residue of a deep and unresolved conflict, or perhaps even some expectation that a woman will inevitably elicit criticism or contempt if she discloses the difficulties that attended her pursuit of a career. Extreme reticence, even self-deprecation, in women of significant accomplishment is so general that it almost constitutes a norm.

Edith Wharton's primary achievements in treating the subject are her subtle comprehension of the conditions that would produce such an attitude and her brilliant ability to present them so that they could be understood by others. *The Touchstone,* published in 1900, was Wharton's first full-length novel, and it is a study of the woman-as-artist—a novel of apprenticeship. Yet its subject is deeply disguised; for like so many other women of genius, Edith Wharton was reluctant to reveal the particularities of her own experience.

At first glance, *The Touchstone* would seem not even to fall into the category of *Künstlerroman,* for its main character is a man named Glennard, and he is not an artist of any kind. There is a woman novelist of significance in the tale, the elusive Margaret Aubyn, and the story opens with a long reference to her (at a point when the novel's apparent "hero" has not yet been introduced); nevertheless, Wharton's portrayal of this woman is so indirect that a reader is, at first, liable to underestimate her importance. To be sure, Margaret Aubyn is "famous," and the events of *her* life, at least, clearly merit examination (we are informed in the first lines of the story that a professor in England is collecting material for a biography of her);

however, because she has already died when the novel begins and because we never hear her voice or read even so much as a word she has written, it seems unlikely that she is to be the principal source of interest in the novel—this ghost, who exists only as the silent inscription on old letters or as the almost-forgotten face among Glennard's outdated photographs. Nonetheless, slowly and stealthily, the force of Margaret Aubyn's character gathers power: everywhere obliquely present, she haunts Glennard's consciousness and shapes his life—becoming, in the end, the major player in this surprising piece of fiction. What we have, then, is *an apprenticeship novel of hide-and-seek,* an ingenious, self-effacing mode of fiction that Edith Wharton devised as one "appropriate" way to address the difficulties of the woman author.

Undoubtedly, even Edith Wharton's ingenuity was challenged by the problem of writing fiction about the woman-as-artist, for she returned to the subject again and again. (During the first fifteen years of her career, she wrote a great many variations on the theme—concluding in 1905 with *The House of Mirth,* whose "artist"-heroine, Lily Bart, invests all of her considerable aesthetic talent in the futile contrivances of self-adornment.) The results were complex and full of insight; indeed, the task of interpreting them may present a considerable challenge to the reader.

To appreciate the many implications of *The Touchstone,* we must understand three different forces that shaped Wharton's experience. First, there was the general condition of all women in late nineteenth-century America—the extraordinary limitations that were placed upon their activities and the mutilating norms of "femininity" that did such injury to their images of self. Second, there was the personal pain of Wharton's own experience as a gifted, ambitious female—the anger and despair of a talented young woman whose artistic genius was condemned at every turn. Finally, there was the accumulated tradition of American literature, the medium in which Wharton wished to work—for even though she was determined to expose the ways in which society had disenfranchised women, Wharton was constrained to begin her revolutionary process by using the literary tools that this culture had provided and by taking account of the success or failure of other women writers who had addressed the problem. It was an heroic task.

The general problem—the handicap that has afflicted women in a majority of cultures throughout history and that has been sustained, fueled, created, and re-created over the course of so many centuries that they constitute millennia—is the assumption that while men are important, women are not. This damaging prejudice becomes a lethal weapon when it is accompanied, as it often is, by an unspoken corollary: men are *intrisically* "better" than women, born to a "superior" condition that females can never even *earn,* no matter what their achievements might be. Today, we have finally begun to understand both the pervasive effects of such assumptions and the subtle, often seductive ways in which they are perpetuated. However, in 1900, when *The Touchstone* was first published, it would have been considered "unnatural" to take the view that women were men's "equal." Edith Jones Wharton, who was born in 1862, grew to maturity in a world almost entirely shaped by a collection of attitudes that devalue women—especially intelligent, artistically gifted, and ambitious women.

The second half of the nineteenth century was a particularly repressive era. Between 1848, when the first Women's Rights Convention was held in Seneca Falls, New York, and 1920, when the Nineteenth Amendment to the Constitution was ratified, issues concerning women's rights were being actively debated, often acrimoniously and sometimes viciously. And the right to vote was only one, rather visible, prerogative at stake; others were perhaps more important in women's everyday lives.

In 1862, married women were still legally barred from holding property in most of the United States: everything, including a woman's books, personal papers, and clothes, belonged to her husband; if a wife should be gainfully employed, her husband had the legal right to her paycheck; if money or property were to be given to a married woman—or if she inherited them—they became the legal property of her husband. If a woman bore children, her husband had absolute legal control over them; and when a woman's husband died, he might leave the guardianship of "his" children to anybody—his family or perhaps his friends—for even when she had been widowed, a mother had no legal rights to her own children.

If she was confronted with a dishonest or abusive husband, a woman *might* take her children and run away (divorce was virtually unobtainable); however, when her husband pursued her, he could take the children back, and if he was vindictive, he was entitled to take back even the clothes his fugitive wife was wearing.

Since single women were in some respects much freer than those who had married, one might suppose that a young woman's desire to wed would be ambivalent at best (and a disinclination to marry would have been powerfully reinforced by several other things—the fact that birth control was generally unavailable, for example, and that childbirth was still a life-threatening ordeal). Thus in certain parts of America, most notably in New England, the status of spinsterhood became a respectable and dignified alternative for those few women with enough inherited money to afford the privilege. Nonetheless, society as a whole was not prepared to approve of such a way of life. There were many ways of making it all but impossible for a woman to live independently of a man; perhaps the most efficient was to deny her a living wage.

Until after the Civil War, no woman who wished to be thought "respectable" sought employment outside the home, and for many decades thereafter, the range of jobs open to them was so narrow that it was all but impossible for a woman to pursue a "career." Women who were forced by poverty to support themselves (and possibly small children or aged parents) confronted a social system that permitted them almost no opportunity to do so. Louisa May Alcott published a novel entitled *Work* in 1873 that is prefaced by a quotation from Carlyle asserting the universal human need for a meaningful job in life: "An endless significance lies in work; in idleness alone is there perpetual despair." Yet Alcott could not restructure the realities of the world, and the possibilities for employment available to her heroine are cruelly limited—actress, teacher, companion, seamstress. These more or less recapitulate the jobs that were available to women in the real world; the only major omission is mill work, backbreaking and life-shortening. The professions—medicine, law, architecture, and the like—were effectively closed to women until well into the twentieth century. Furthermore, even opportunities for higher education were stringently limited. Females were not given the tools for a career of any kind because they were not supposed to seek one; and if, somehow, they did achieve success in some profession, they were obliged to cope with the pervasive assumption that there must be something strange about them, something unnatural. This was, perhaps, the most onerous burden of all.

It has always been the case that America's myths, the stories that have been judged "interesting" or "worthwhile" or even just "fun," overwhelmingly feature a white male hero; our notions of social order and "culture" are built upon such tales—the valor and honesty of George Washington, the success of Horatio Alger, the pioneering courage of Davy Crockett or Daniel Boone, the carefree adventurousness of Tom Sawyer or Huck

Finn. Women's appropriate role has been defined as no more than the supporting player in such stories. Even worse, women have been told "how women feel"—and "how women *ought* to feel"—by men. Never was this more the case than during the latter half of the nineteenth century.

Women's "proper realm" was the home, where Mother ruled as a goddess of the hearth—patient, generous, kind, and selfless. "Good" women ("normal" women) were assumed to be almost entirely without the capacity for rage; their "innate" mode of behavior was judged to be passive rather than active. The nineteenth-century novelist Elizabeth Stuart Phelps captures the stereotype well in her satiric essay "The True Woman," published in 1871.

> The "true woman," we are told, desires and seeks no noisy political existence. To the "true woman" the whirr and bustle of public life are unattractive. A "true woman" honors the homely virtues and appreciates the quiet dignities of household life. She is not a "true woman" who cannot find in the "sweet, safe corner . . . behind the heads of children" scope for her activities and content[ment] in her adjustment to them. A "true woman" will shrink from the rough contact of the world. The "true woman" instinctively merges her life—social, political, commercial—in that of her husband.

Moreover, though affectionate towards husband and children, a "true woman" was assumed to be entirely devoid of sexual passion. Perhaps nothing captures America's ethical expectations for women better than certain colossal art works—the Statue of Liberty or the blindfolded Justice holding a balance scale—imposing females who embody "virtue" in patient silence and powerless immobility.

Recognizing these constraints upon women's lives in nineteenth-century America can surely help us to amplify our understanding of *The Touchstone:* for example, Alexa Trent's relatively passive acceptance of the "poverty and misfortune" that had "overhung her childhood" is less a sign of personal weakness than a realistic reaction to the fact that there were so few opportunities for women to obtain gainful employment; and the extremity of Margaret Aubyn's emotional vulnerability becomes poignant and clear when we realize that she could never have obtained a divorce to escape her "conspicuously unhappy marriage." Wharton was not obliged to belabor such facts because they were a "given" of the culture in 1900.

Other problems of gender, however, were not a matter of public knowledge. Few readers would have known what obstacles and uncertainties confronted an ambitious woman writer. These are the dilemmas conventionally examined in a *Künstlerroman;* to the extent that the plight of a gifted woman writer mirrors the circumstances of *all* talented women, these are the quandaries that intelligent readers would most urgently wish to have examined. Yet it is here that Wharton is deliberately oblique in *The Touchstone.* More than three decades later, she published an autobiography in which she disclosed some of her early unhappiness; other, more intimate, recollections were discovered among the unpublished notebooks and letters after her death. And all of these taken together can help us to penetrate the strategies of concealment that characterize this unusual novel of apprenticeship.

Her mother and father, Lucretia and Frederick Jones, were prominent, well-to-do New Yorkers—"cultured" people with a vigorous respect for precise and graceful language. During her youth, Wharton traveled abroad extensively with her parents while her brothers, who were both considerably older than she, pursued the Ivy League education that was routinely expected of all young men of their class. It was a background with much that might be useful to an aspiring writer; however, this inheritance was sorely compromised in Edith Wharton's case by issues of gender.

Perhaps the dominant strain in Wharton's memories of her childhood and youth is her passion for beauty: she had a photographic, visual memory and was so susceptible to her surroundings that ugliness or squalor produced an almost physical revulsion in her. Her love of language was an extension of this passion for beauty: "I was enthralled by *words*," she wrote in her diaries.

> It mattered very little whether I understood them or not: the sound was the essential thing. Wherever I went, they sang to me like the birds in an enchanted forest. And they had *looks* as well as sound: each one had its own gestures and physiognomy.

What were dolls to a child who had such marvellous toys . . . ?

Even Wharton's earliest memories reveal the desire to take a hand in *creating* the beauty that she responded to with such intensity: "I always saw the visible world as a series of pictures . . . and [I wanted] *to make the picture prettier.*" That is, she wanted to become an artist. Yet simply because she was a girl (and not a boy), her aspiration was almost ruinously compromised.

During this period of American Victorianism, unless a woman had inherited a fortune, her "value" was almost entirely a function of her outward appearance, her beauty: intelligence need not necessarily be a detriment, and a certain ethical seriousness could seem appropriately "feminine" if it was attractively focused upon issues that pertained to chastity and motherhood. There was a pervasive, naive conviction that in women, all excellence of character would surely be manifested in visible personal beauty. An enterprising man of genius might become a "self-made" man. A woman might become better-dressed, more graceful, more exquisitely groomed; however, she could never in the same sense be self-made—although she could, by artfully enhancing her beauty, "marry well." It went without saying that no respectable female aspired to become an artist. Society had decreed that in women such talent was to be focused entirely upon their personal appearance and their domestic surroundings. Women did not *create* beauty. Women *were* beautiful.

Thus it was that Edith Wharton's earliest artistic stirrings were transformed into the desire "to look pretty." As a mature woman in her sixties, Wharton could finally understand the confusion: "I really believe it has always been an aesthetic desire, rather than a form of vanity." However, during most of her early life, this displacement of artistic passion resulted in immeasurable pain. Perhaps no incident is so poignant as Wharton's recollection of her first meetings with the distinguished novelist Henry James (who was later to become her most valued colleague).

> Old friends of my husband's . . . asked us to dine with Henry James. I could hardly believe that such a privilege could befall me, and I could think of only one way of deserving it—to put on my newest Doucet dress, and try to look my prettiest! I was probably not more than twenty-five, those were the principles in which I had been brought up, and it would never have occurred to me that I had anything to commend me to the man whose shoe-strings I thought myself unworthy to unloose. I can see the dress still—and it *was* pretty. . . . But alas, it neither gave me the courage to speak, nor attracted the attention of the great man.
>
> A year or two later . . . the same opportunity came my way. . . . Once more I thought: How can I make myself pretty enough for him to notice me? Well—this time I had a new hat: *a beautiful new hat!* . . . But he noticed neither the hat nor its

wearer—and the second of our meetings fell as flat
as the first.

Wharton could remember moments like these without
bitterness. Yet there was a darker, more tragic component
in the gendered injunctions that had distorted her judgment: the mandate to *be* beautiful instead of *creating*
beauty had produced such conflict and confusion in Wharton's life that during her years of apprenticeship there
were long periods when she was too depressed to write.
As a result, the author who eventually became a woman
of immense energy and remarkable productivity did not
publish her first novel (*The Touchstone*) until she was almost forty and had already lost more than a decade of
creative time.

Wharton was far from unique in experiencing this
kind of disabling conflict. Her contemporary, the economic theorist Charlotte Perkins Gilman, based her brilliant short story "The Yellow Wallpaper" (1890) on an
emotional crisis that bears uncanny resemblances to Wharton's own malaise. Moreover, both drew the same conclusion from their experience: every woman must have the
right to engage in intellectually fulfilling work; idleness
and passivity are not luxuries—they are invitations to mental instability. In Edith Wharton's life, this conviction (reinforced by adult experience) had deep roots.

Books had always provided an "escape from [the op-
pression of] chronic moral malady" and reading and writing had been a source of health—a reliable weapon against
depression. Yet Wharton's parents had no sympathy what-

soever for the girl's deep need; instead, they were stirred to a vague but fixed suspicion of her literary inclinations, and they imposed stringent rules upon her progress through fiction.

> My mother, perplexed by the discovery that she had produced an omnivorous reader, and not knowing how to direct [this] reading . . . turned the difficulty by reviving a rule of her own school-room days, and decreeing that I should never read a novel without asking her permission. I was a painfully conscientious child and, conforming literally to this decree, I submitted to her every work of fiction which attracted my fancy.

In fact, Wharton obeyed the injunction until her own marriage, at the age of twenty-three.

Even more stringent prohibitions were put upon her writing. The little girl had begun to compose stories virtually as soon as she could put words upon the page, and by the time she was eight or nine, writing had become perhaps her most cherished activity (she attempted her first "novel" at the age of eleven). Yet her parents sought actively to discourage the unladylike aberration of literary composition. They had a simple recourse: they gave her only a pauper's portion of the necessary tools.

> It was not thought necessary to feed my literary ambitions with foolscap, and for lack of paper I was driven to begging for the wrappings of the parcels

delivered at the house. After a while these were regarded as belonging to me, and I always kept a stack in my room.

The future novelist worked on the floor, covering "vast expanses of wrapping paper with prose and verse." There was no one to read this work—no way of judging its merit, no way of obtaining suggestions for its improvement, and certainly no source of encouragement. "How could I ever have supposed I could be an author?" she exclaimed fifty years later, "I had never even seen one in the flesh!"

At length, an apparently decisive halt was put to the entire process: "When I was seventeen my parents decided that I spent too much time in reading, and that I was to come out a year before the accepted age." Laced into pale green brocade—with her red hair piled high upon her head and a gigantic bouquet of lilies of the valley in her hands—she became a debutante. There was no mistaking the implicit command of this ritual in old New York. For the next ten years, Edith Wharton ceased composing fiction altogether.

A modern reader may wonder at the girl's docility; yet it is well to recollect the general condition of disempowerment that all women still confronted: far from ignorant, Wharton had nonetheless never attended school; she was not equipped in any way to support herself. Furthermore, if she had struck out on her own, her action would have been perceived as bizarre—even insane—for society thought that "normal" women would want only one occupation, the management of a husband's home.

Most debilitating of all, she entered adult life with very little self-confidence. Because she was "different" from most girls and young women, she had been subjected to a barrage of criticism at home, and this ridicule had thoroughly demoralized her. The two sons, who occupied a privileged position in the family, were enlisted in the process of putting the precocious daughter "in her place."

> I was laughed at by my brothers for my red hair, and for the supposed abnormal size of my hands and feet; and as I was much the least good-looking of the family, the consciousness of my physical short-comings was heightened by the beauty of the persons about me. My parents—or at least my mother— laughed at me for using "long words," and for caring for dress (in which, heaven knows, she set me the example!); and under this perpetual cross-fire of criticism I became a painfully shy, self-conscious child.

She was accused of having less "heart" than her brothers, and her desire to become an author was treated like some distasteful form of deviance. "I cannot hope to render the tone in which my mother pronounced the names of [women authors such as] Mrs. Beecher Stowe, who was so 'common' yet so successful." Gradually, Wharton learned to protect herself by concealing her literary activity from everyone: "The child knows instinctively when it will be understood, and . . . I kept my adventures with books to myself." Having learned the protective value of reticence and self-effacement, she could never entirely lose the habit of them, and even after she had become an internationally respected and successful novelist, Edith Wharton was afflicted with an almost morbid shyness—remaining aloof and diffident unless she was among trusted friends.

Clearly Wharton's own apprenticeship had given her enough material for a powerful *Künstlerroman*. Indeed, some such work *seems* a "natural" first step, a way of confronting the mocking ghosts of the past and putting them to rest. The major tradition in American fiction had already produced examples of the genre—most notably from Wharton's point of view, perhaps, Henry James's *Roderick Hudson*—and by 1900 an era of intense interest in just such novels had recently begun. The next two decades would see the publication of D. H. Lawrence's *Sons and Lovers,* James Joyce's *A Portrait of the Artist as a Young Man,* and F. Scott Fitzgerald's *The Far Side of Paradise.* Yet for many reasons, Wharton never drew upon the particulars of her own life to write such a work; and when, years later (in 1929 and 1931), she wrote two novels about a struggling writer, her protagonist was a man, whose hardships bore scant resemblance to her own. There were excellent reasons for her reticence, and many derived from her wary observation of the way other American women's work had been received when they dared to discuss the difficulties of the female artist and drew autobiographically upon their own experience to do so.

During the nineteenth century in America, two well-known novels of a woman's apprenticeship had been published: *Ruth Hall* (1854) by Fanny Fern and *The Story of Avis* (1877) by Elizabeth Stuart Phelps. Although Edith Wharton would have judged these works to be far below the literary standard set by women such as George Eliot or Jane Austen, both were interesting pieces of fiction. However, neither was of much use to her as a model; for instead of establishing a usable pattern upon which she might draw, both novels had become the target of such cruel and belittling criticism that to follow their example closely would be to invite a hostile attitude toward her own work even before a chapter of it had been read. The "tradition" of the female *Künstlerroman* in America, then, functioned primarily to instruct Edith Wharton in what *not* to do. Even this, however, proved an invaluable lesson.

Ruth Hall (subtitled *A Domestic Tale of the Present Time*) is more an account of male perfidy than it is a study of its heroine's artistic development. Ruth's father is an unprincipled miser who pushes her into marriage at the age of sixteen merely to relieve himself of the financial burden of her upkeep. Ruth loves her husband deeply, and he treats her with great affection and kindness; however, when he dies, his own family is so unrelievedly mean-tempered that they refuse to contribute anything to help Ruth and her two children. In desperation, the widow attempts to make her own way, but she is thwarted by the fact that there are no jobs for women that pay enough to support a mother and two children, no matter how meagerly they are willing to live. Finally, when she is on the point of starvation, Ruth Hall begins to write for the public press, and eventually she becomes successful enough to take care of her small family—this, despite the fact that male authors, male editors, and male readers have exhibited hostility towards this "uppity" woman. Before the novel's end, Ruth has met a "good man" who wants to marry her; however, she is not willing—yet—to relinquish the sweet pleasure of being entirely in command of her own destiny without having to rely upon a man.

Ruth Hall is saturated with the heroine's love for her children (an acceptable passion in any nineteenth-century mother), yet the novel bristles with anger, too: the outrage is not for talent ignored, but for men who appropriate all power and systematically belittle women while they shamelessly exploit them. It would have been impossible to miss the feminist intensity of this message, and the critics responded to the work like a pack of bulls tormented by a bee. One wrote in the *New York Times,*

> If Fanny Fern were a man . . . who believed that the gratification of revenge were a proper occupation for one who has been abused, and that those who have injured us are fair game, *Ruth Hall* would be a natural and excusable book. But we confess that we cannot understand how a delicate, suffering woman can hunt down even her persecutors so remorselessly. We cannot think so highly of [such] an author's womanly gentleness.

Critics claimed that the heroine was suffused by an "irreverence for things sacred" and that the author was no more than a woman of "a certain age" who should learn to "kiss the rod" that had afflicted her—a creature of "unfemininely bitter wrath and spite."

The hostile reviewers of this novel put together an argument that was as hypnotic as it was self-contradictory. "True women" didn't have the kind of feelings that were revealed in this work; thus the heroine could not be "normal"—certainly the author was not "normal"—and readers should simply dismiss the novel from their minds. "Decent women"—"normal women"—wrote sentimental novels that extolled the virtues of home and hearth. Of course, most "true men" find such novels boring; in fact, they are generally "inferior" novels. But of course, "normal women" *do* write "inferior" novels.

All of this controversy took place just before Edith Wharton was born; however, the lesson of it remained a powerful legend in American fiction, becoming part of Wharton's immediate literary inheritance. The controversy highlighted a baffling, maddening dilemma: after she had decided to become an author, Edith Wharton was determined to write powerful, first-rate fiction; she also intended to be thought of as a perfectly "normal," decent woman. Given the evidence presented by this literary inheritance, how could she (or any other talented female author) achieve such a goal? Elizabeth Stuart Phelps's female *Künstlerroman* did nothing to make the situation simpler.

When *The Story of Avis* was published in 1877, Wharton was fifteen. If she had asked her mother's permission to read it at the time (and there is no indication that she did), it would surely have been withheld, for *The Story of Avis* was roundly denounced in terms that the castigation of *Ruth Hall* had already made familiar. In a review that was typical of many, *Harper's New Monthly Magazine* declared, "We can not think that such a novel . . . is altogether a wholesome story. . . . The passion may not be untrue to nature altogether, but it is at least open to question whether this is the kind of interior experience which it is desireable that our young girls should have portrayed before them as the ideal of true love." The "undesireable passion" in question was nothing other than a woman's commitment to creating art and her determination to have a marriage that supported this vocation.

Avis Dobell, the daughter of a professor in a small New England town, is a brilliant young painter who has decided never to marry. She does not hate men—is not even indifferent to them; however, she does recognize that marriage may be incompatible with a woman's desire to become an artist. Thus when Avis falls in love with Philip Ostrander, she at first refuses his proposal, saying that she "cannot accept the consequences of love as other women do." Slowly, however, time and circumstance weaken her resolve. When at last she protests that "I have my work, and I have my life. I was not made to yield these to any man," he responds, "Only let us love, and live, and work together. Your genius shall be more tenderly my pride than my little talents can possibly be yours. . . . Try me if you will; trust me if you can." And she does. The last two-thirds of the novel deal more with marriage than with art. The duties of keeping house, the obligations of child-rearing, the burden of bearing the jealousy and petty vindictiveness of a husband whose talent is lesser than her own—all of these conspire at first to make Avis miserable and at length to break her health and subvert her talent. By the novel's conclusion, even widowhood is not sufficient to restore enough vitality so that she can resume her vocation.

Phelps's novel does not criticize particular men (as Fanny Fern had done); instead, it sets forth a bleak indictment of the belief that all women must seek happiness and fulfillment exclusively within a domestic sphere. Indeed, the excellence of *The Story of Avis* derives not so much from its "literary" qualities as from the power of its social criticism.

An accomplished essayist, Elizabeth Stuart Phelps made numerous succinct and compelling comments about women's role in American society, many of which may be found in her scathing essay "The True Woman," published in 1871.

> Every time that a man assumes to indicate to a woman the character of her "sphere" he offers her an insult. To use that homely phrase which has no graceful counterpart, it is none of his business what her sphere is.

27

Woman is not man's ward. Man is not woman's guardian. Man is incapable, even if he were called upon to do so, of competently judging for woman in the adjustment of her "place" in society. . . .

. . . nobody knows as yet what the womanly character is. Our ideals of it are, *par excellence,* fictitious and contingent.

Although this is a compelling indictment, Phelps was realistic enough to recognize how arduous a task it would be to change the world. Thus the narrator of *The Story of Avis* acknowledges, "We have been told that it takes three generations to make a gentleman: we may believe that it will take as much, or more, to make A WOMAN." In the end, *The Story of Avis* is less a female *Künstlerroman* than a novel of social protest. Nonetheless, both the novel itself and its critical reception were immensely instructive to Edith Wharton, whose own fiction would combine a sensitive examination of women's lives with clear-eyed, impassioned social criticism.

More than a dozen years passed between the time Wharton left her mother's home to get married and the time when she wrote *The Touchstone,* and this was a period of comprehensive "self-education." Her knowledge of fiction—American, English, and Continental—became encyclopedic. She was attentive to technique (and kept a notebook containing some of her observations); but in addition to studying the craft of fiction, she looked for female writers whose experience might help her fashion her own work. The lesson taught by Fern and Phelps was discouraging, but nonetheless instructive.

It was clear that although a male author could write a novel about the anguish of his struggles to become an author, no woman author could emulate this example with impunity. A woman wasn't supposed to become an artist (she wasn't even supposed to want to become an artist); if she suffered in the process of trying, that was only "normal" (or worse, "deserved"), and any straightforward account of her suffering was liable to be ridiculed or condemned. A woman novelist who wished to write a *Künstlerroman* would have to discover new ways to deal with the plight of the female artist.

From Fanny Fern's experience, Wharton learned that to the extent that men were to be criticized for their insensitivity to women's plight (at best) or their callousness and cruelty to women (at worst), the approach could not be direct. Neither narrator nor heroine could engage in an overt attack, for too many readers would have a negative reaction to any indictment that had been framed in such an open way. There might be justice in attacking the male establishment; there was certainly satisfaction to be had from a righteous expression of rage. However, these tactics contained the potential for self-defeat. If obtuse and uncaring men were to be censured for their treatment of women, the negative judgment must originate with the reader herself or himself. Righteous rage must "belong" to the reader; only under these conditions would it be accepted.

Wharton learned another kind of lesson from Elizabeth Stuart Phelps. Didactic, explicit social criticism can work against the novel's most effective power. A novel can make a reader "feel" a situation; insofar as a novel "lectures" its audience, readers are apt to stop empathizing with its heroine. Edith Wharton had no illusions about the society in which she lived; she saw its moral deficiencies and emotional injustices. "There it was before me," she wrote in her autobiography,

> in all its flatness and futility. . . . The problem was how to extract from such a subject the typical human significance which is the story-teller's reason for telling one story rather than another. In what aspect could a society of irresponsible pleasure-seekers be said to have, on the "old woe of the world," any deeper bearing than the people composing such a society could guess? The answer was that a frivolous society can acquire dramatic significance only through what its frivolity destroys. Its tragic implication lies in its power of debasing people and ideals.

The superior logic of an argument will not stir the reader's indignation. However, when a reader *feels* the full tragic implication of society's mistakes, this intimate horror might well provoke moral indignation. Such is the premise that informs all of Edith Wharton's most powerfully satiric fiction, and *The Touchstone* represents her first full-length exploration of the method.

In some respects, the ultimate target of Wharton's attack was much more sweeping than that of either Fern or Phelps. Many of the obstacles confronted by Ruth Hall and Avis Dobell had been monetary; while there was no doubt that the economic constraints society had placed upon women could be crippling, it was equally true that these were not the worst obstacles women had to face. Many of the objective problems that Fern and Phelps had examined in their fiction would have been less troublesome if their heroines had only had a good deal more money (because household help and baby-nurses could have provided them with a measure of free time); nonetheless, as Edith Wharton knew from her own experience, even with money enough to provide ample access to such forms of freedom, the woman artist would still confront enormous obstacles. In some respects, then, the deepest and most intractable problems of the talented and ambitious woman could be explored only by moving beyond these "circumstantial" obstacles. (Wharton makes this point quite explicitly in a short story entitled "The Pelican," which takes up the dilemma of "the mother" in *Ruth Hall* and introduces an ironic variation into it.)

The most mutilating constraints upon women are invisible: they lie in notions of the "normal" woman as essentially passive and intellectually indifferent; they are reinforced by the expectation that a "sane" and "healthy" woman will want no role beyond the domestic world; and they are enacted by the cruel dismissal of gifted or ambitious women as "unfeminine" or "unnatural." Sometimes, these constraints are enforced by men who want to keep women "in their place." Yet sometimes they are perpetuated by women themselves, who have internalized these assumptions (this was the most painful lesson of Edith Wharton's own experience). Women may believe that they will compromise their "femininity" by seeking intellectual fulfillment; women may fear success, sometimes even more than they desire it; women may be wracked with conflict, sometimes entirely immobilized by it. And most crippling of all, women may believe that they must never reveal their uncertainty and anguish—and that if they do attain "success," they must treat it in such a matter-of-fact way that the hardships of their struggle remain entirely invisible.

Thus, writing a "female" *Künstlerroman* could be almost a test of sorts, a challenge to the woman author to set an example for others by having the courage to confront her own most painful fears and the ingenuity to discover a way of disclosing them.

There is no certain way to know where Edith Wharton got the central notion for her extraordinary solution to the dilemma; however, her notebooks reveal that she was reading the work of the French novelist Stendhal with great care during these years of apprenticeship. Stendhal was a superb craftsman, and his work merited the study of any serious novelist; however, he could be capable of insufferable viciousness where women writers were concerned. "A woman must never write anything but posthumous works," he declared in a well-known "witty" remark. "For a woman under fifty to get into print is submitting her happiness to the most terrible of lotteries; if she has the good fortune to have a lover, she'll begin by losing him." This was precisely the kind of wounding decree that Wharton had heard as a child and young woman; now, however, she was prepared to respond by taking the premise of Stendhal's venomous joke and fashioning a piece of fiction around it, breathing life into the paradoxical notion of a woman writing for "posthumous" publication. She constructed her counterattack with great care.

Like a guerrilla warrior, Wharton approaches the reader through a series of revelations and partial concealments that simultaneously disclose and disguise the presence of a "woman author." Thus, despite the unusual opening of the story—a paragraph from a newspaper seeking information about the recently deceased "famous novelist," Mrs. Aubyn—there is every reason to suppose that Glennard is to be the novel's principal character, perhaps even its "hero." And Glennard is so fixedly preoccupied with the problem of getting enough money to be married that the reader may be as uninterested in Mrs. Aubyn's nature as he clearly is. Only upon a second reading, perhaps, does one notice the "boredom" and "resentment" that shape Glennard's sensibilities: emotionally stingy and inclined to employ metaphors of money-making with regard to every human activity, he scarcely warrants our trust. His response to the newspaper passage about Margaret Aubyn, for example, is condescending and self-serving:

> He saw her again as she had looked at their first
> meeting, the poor woman of genius with her long
> pale face and short-sighted eyes, softened a little by
> the grace of youth and inexperience, but so incapa-
> ble even then of any hold upon the pulses.

This is little more than a judgmental stereotype with which
most of us are already familiar: the "poor woman of genius"—not pretty, not graceful, not feminine—emotionally needy, perhaps, but certainly not *lovable.*

Even though Glennard's reminiscences continue at
some length, they resound with a curious emptiness: we
learn almost nothing about Margaret Aubyn, for his attention is focused entirely upon himself, his "vanity" finding
"a retrospective enjoyment in the sentiment his heart had
rejected." It is ghoulish, but perhaps not surprising, that
his mind slides so smoothly into the predatory mode.
What does he stand *to make* out of his relationship with
Margaret Aubyn; how can he *profit* from her unrequited
passion? Little by little, then, the newspaper quotation
with which the tale has opened—a request for "information" about the "famous . . . Mrs. Aubyn"—seems to
articulate the reader's need: as the tale progresses, we
understand that the "real" Margaret Aubyn is not contained in Glennard's memories, and we may begin to hope
for a citation from her fiction or a passage snatched from
a letter, anything that will provide the explicit, circumstantial detail that he seems unable to conjure. In the end,
The Touchstone makes as strong a case on behalf of the

woman artist as either of its predecessors; however, while the heroines of *Ruth Hall* and *The Story of Avis* demanded our support by their impassioned presence, Margaret Aubyn wins us through her absence. And she is not alone in this triumph, for *The Touchstone* also suggests a new age of cooperative support among women.

One of the most poignant moments in *The Story of Avis* occurs when the heroine is visited by a woman that her husband had courted and then discarded. There is no more than a brief, unsatisfactory conversation between them before the woman turns to go. Yet she does not leave without protesting her loneliness.

> "I don't know *why* I came," she said rather pitifully. "Why does a woman trust herself to do anything, when she's beside herself with things she can't speak of? That's the worst of being a woman. What you go through can't be told. It isn't respectable for one woman to tell another what she has to bear."

The narrator comments, "We hear much of the jealousy and scorn of women among themselves. It is not often that we are reminded of the . . . generous devotion which renders the relation of woman to woman one of the most subtle in the world." In Phelps's novel, this momentary meeting, so pregnant with possibility, comes to very little. Indeed, the chief woman-to-woman relationship, Avis's friendship with Coy Bishop, is more competitive than cooperative: Coy is quite satisfied with woman's traditional role, and although she finds Avis's plight lamentable, she neither understands her nor empathizes with her.

By comparison, the importance of women's mutual sympathy and support is central to *The Touchstone.* Alexa Trent is not an artist in the narrow sense: she does not write books or paint pictures. Yet her role in creating a place for "the woman author" is as important as Margaret Aubyn's. Although Alexa's given name carries associations of law and regulation, her presence in the novel very often has an altogether different implication: she is associated with images of birth and growth, and it is this generative capacity that she shares deeply with Margaret Aubyn. Midway through the novel, Glennard comes upon her while she is reading one of Mrs. Aubyn's fictions entitled *Pomegranate Seed.* Although Wharton's allusion to this tale of Demeter and Persephone is glancing, its significance is not meant to be overlooked.

Feminists today have noted that alone of ancient myths, the story of Demeter and Persephone recounts an archetypal example of women's unique power. Confronted by loss or absence, female force confers the capacity to revive life in the face of apparent death. This myth celebrates attachment and continuation, not competition and conflict; indeed, it shows that these are fundamental to the sustaining of life itself. Clearly, in some way Alexa Trent and Margaret Aubyn reenact the generative message of this myth, though the specific role played by each is deliberately blurred. Both are, in some sense, "artists," and yet, in some sense, both also "give birth." Ultimately, they cooperate to redeem Glennard and to correct the reader's notions of a woman's "proper" role.

There is one vexingly undisclosed secret in this novel: Margaret Aubyn. Did she love Glennard deeply? Was she heartbroken by his indifference; was she, perhaps, indignant—even enraged? And why *did* she leave America to live abroad? Was the attitude of her countrymen towards a gifted and successful woman artist intolerably oppressive? In choosing not to provide the answers to such questions, Edith Wharton forces each reader to form his or her own notion of the woman and her feelings. And then, as if to make up for Margaret Aubyn's absence, Edith Wharton insinuates an image of "the author" into this book.

The newspaper clipping at the beginning of the novel (seeking information about a deceased woman novelist) is balanced at the conclusion of the novel by a group of quotations from newspaper reviews of Edith Wharton's own earlier short stories. Acting almost like a coda, they reassure us that the very-much-alive "Mrs. Wharton" combines skill and success with social grace—in short, that she is both a female novelist and a "normal" woman. And with these exit-lines, Edith Wharton undoubtedly hoped to end the disparagement and hostility that had beset women novelists for half a century.

THE TOUCHSTONE

BY EDITH WHARTON
AUTHOR OF THE
GREATER INCLINATION

CHARLES SCRIBNER'S
SONS, NEW YORK: 1900

1

Professor Joslin, who, as our readers are doubtless aware, is engaged in writing the life of Mrs. Aubyn, asks us to state that he will be greatly indebted to any of the famous novelist's friends who will furnish him with information concerning the period previous to her coming to England. Mrs. Aubyn had so few intimate friends, and consequently so few regular correspondents, that letters will be of special value. Professor Joslin's address is 10 Augusta Gardens, Kensington, and he begs us to say that he will promptly return any documents entrusted to him.

G lennard dropped the *Spectator* and sat looking into the fire. The club was filling up, but he still had to himself the small inner room with its darkening outlook down the rain-streaked prospect of Fifth Avenue. It was all dull and dismal enough, yet a moment earlier his boredom had been perversely tinged by a sense of resentment at the thought that, as things were going, he might in time have to surrender even the despised privilege of boring himself within those particular four walls. It was not that he cared much for the club, but that the remote contingency of having to give it up stood to him, just then, perhaps by very reason of its insignificance and remoteness, for the symbol of his increasing abnegations; of that perpetual paring-off that was gradually reducing existence to the naked business of keeping himself alive. It was the futility of his multiplied shifts and privations that made them seem unworthy of a high attitude—the sense that, however rapidly he eliminated the superfluous, his cleared horizon was likely to offer no nearer view of the one prospect toward which he strained. To give up things in order to marry the woman one loves is easier than to give them up without being brought appreciably nearer to such a conclusion.

Through the open door he saw young Hollingsworth rise with a yawn from the ineffectual solace of a brandy-and-soda and transport his purposeless person to the window. Glennard measured his course with a contemptuous eye. It was so like Hollingsworth to get up and look out of the window just as it was growing too dark to see anything! There was a man rich enough to do what he pleased—had he been capable of being pleased—yet barred from all conceivable achievement by his own impervious dulness; while, a few feet off, Glennard, who wanted only enough to keep a decent coat on his back and a roof over the head of the woman he loved—Glennard, who had sweated, toiled, denied himself for the scant measure of opportunity that his zeal would have converted into a kingdom—sat wretchedly calculating that, even when he had resigned from the club, and knocked off his cigars, and given up his Sundays out of town, he would still be no nearer to attainment.

The *Spectator* had slipped to his feet, and as he picked it up his eye fell again on the paragraph addressed to the friends of Mrs. Aubyn. He had read it for the first time with a scarcely perceptible quickening of attention: her name had so long been public property that his eye passed it unseeingly, as the crowd in the street hurries without a glance by some familiar monument.

"Information concerning the period previous to her coming to England. . . ." The words were an evocation. He saw her again as she had looked at their first meeting, the poor woman of genius with her long pale face and short-sighted eyes, softened a little by the grace of youth and inexperience, but so incapable even then of any hold upon the pulses. When she spoke, indeed, she was wonderful, more wonderful, perhaps, than when later, to Glennard's fancy at least, the consciousness of memorable things uttered seemed to take from even her most intimate speech the perfect bloom of privacy. It was in those earliest days, if ever, that he had come near loving her; though even then his sentiment had lived only in the intervals of its expression. Later, when to be loved by her had been a state to touch any man's imagination, the physical reluctance had, inexplicably, so overborne the intellectual attraction, that the last years had been, to both of them, an agony of conflicting impulses. Even now, if, in turning over old papers his hand lit on her letters, the touch filled him with inarticulate misery. . . .

"She had so few intimate friends . . . that letters will be of special value." So few intimate friends! For years she had had but one; one who in the last years had requited her wonderful pages, her tragic outpourings of love, humility and pardon, with the scant phrases by which a man evades the vulgarest of sentimental importunities. He had been a brute in spite of himself, and sometimes, now that the remembrance of her face had faded, and only her voice and words remained with him, he chafed at his own inadequacy, his stupid inability to rise to the height of her passion. His egoism was not of a kind to mirror its complacency in the adventure. To have been loved by the most brilliant woman of her day, and to have been incapable of loving her, seemed to him, in looking back, derisive evidence of his limitations; and his remorseful tenderness for her memory was complicated with a sense of irritation against her for having given him once for all the measure of his emotional capacity. It was not often, however, that he thus probed the past. The public, in taking possession of Mrs. Aubyn, had eased his shoulders of their burden. There was something fatuous in an attitude of sentimental apology toward a memory already classic: to reproach one's self for not having loved Margaret Aubyn was a good deal like being disturbed by an inability to admire the Venus of Milo. From her cold niche of fame she looked down ironically enough on his self-flagellations. . . . It was only when he came on something that belonged to her that he felt a sudden renewal of the old feeling, the strange dual impulse that drew him to her voice but drove him from her hand, so that even now, at sight of anything she had touched, his heart contracted painfully. It happened seldom nowadays. Her little presents, one by one, had disappeared from his rooms, and her letters, kept from some unacknowledged puerile vanity in the possession of such treasures, seldom came beneath his hand. . . .

"Her letters will be of special value—" Her letters! Why, he must have hundreds of them—enough to fill a volume. Sometimes it used to seem to him that they came with every post—he used to avoid looking in his letter-box when he came home to his rooms—but her writing seemed to spring out at him as he put his key in the door.

He stood up and strolled into the other room. Hollingsworth, lounging away from the window, had joined himself to a languidly convivial group of men, to whom, in phrases as halting as though they struggled to define an ultimate idea, he was expounding the cursed nuisance of living in a hole with such a damned climate that one had to get out of it by February, with the contingent difficulty of there being no place to take one's yacht to in winter but that other played-out hole, the Riviera. From the outskirts of this group Glennard wandered to another, where a voice as different as possible from Hollingsworth's colorless organ dominated another circle of languid listeners.

"Come and hear Dinslow talk about his patent: admission free," one of the men sang out in a tone of mock resignation.

Dinslow turned to Glennard the confident pugnacity of his smile. "Give it another six months and it'll be talking about itself," he declared. "It's pretty nearly articulate now."

"Can it say papa?" someone else inquired.

Dinslow's smile broadened. "You'll be deuced glad to say papa to *it* a year from now," he retorted. "It'll be able to support even you in affluence. Look here, now, just let me explain to you—"

Glennard moved away impatiently. The men at the club—all but those who were "in it"—were proverbially "tired" of Dinslow's patent, and none more so than Glennard, whose knowledge of its merits made it loom large in the depressing catalogue of lost opportunities. The relations between the two men had always been friendly, and Dinslow's urgent offers to "take him in on the ground floor" had of late intensified Glennard's sense of his own inability to meet good luck half-way. Some of the men who had paused to listen were already in evening clothes, others on their way home to dress; and Glennard, with an accustomed twinge of humiliation, said to himself that if he lingered among them it was in the miserable hope that one of the number might ask him to dine. Miss Trent had told him that she was to go to the opera that evening with her rich aunt; and if he should have the luck to pick up a dinner invitation he might join her there without extra outlay.

He moved about the room, lingering here and there in a tentative affectation of interest; but though the men greeted him pleasantly, no one asked him to dine. Doubtless they were all engaged, these men who could afford to pay for their dinners, who did not have to hunt for invitations as a beggar rummages for a crust in an ash-barrel! But no—as Hollingsworth left the lessening circle about the table, an admiring youth called out, "Holly, stop and dine!"

Hollingsworth turned on him the crude countenance that looked like the wrong side of a more finished face. "Sorry I can't. I'm in for a beastly banquet."

Glennard threw himself into an arm-chair. Why go home in the rain to dress? It was folly to take a cab to the opera, it was worse folly to go there at all. His perpetual meetings with Alexa Trent were as unfair to the girl as they were unnerving to himself. Since he couldn't marry her, it was time to stand aside and give a better man the chance—and his thought admitted the ironical implication that in the terms of expediency the phrase might stand for Hollingsworth.

2

*H*e dined alone and walked home to his rooms in the
rain. As he turned into Fifth Avenue he caught the
wet gleam of carriages on their way to the opera, and he
took the first side street, in a moment of irritation against
the petty restrictions that thwarted every impulse. It was
ridiculous to give up the opera, not because one might
possibly be bored there, but because one must pay for the
experiment.

In his sitting-room, the tacit connivance of the inani-
mate had centred the lamplight on a photograph of Alexa
Trent, placed, in the obligatory silver frame, just where,
as memory officiously reminded him, Margaret Aubyn's
picture had long throned in its stead. Miss Trent's features
cruelly justified the usurpation. She had the kind of beauty
that comes of a happy accord of face and spirit. It is not
given to many to have the lips and eyes of their rarest
mood, and some women go through life behind a mask

expressing only their anxiety about the butcher's bill or their inability to see a joke. With Miss Trent, face and mind had the same high serious contour. She looked like a throned Justice by some grave Florentine painter; and it seemed to Glennard that her most salient attribute, or that at least to which her conduct gave most consistent expression, was a kind of passionate justness—the intuitive feminine justness that is so much rarer than a reasoned impartiality. Circumstances had tragically combined to develop this instinct into a conscious habit. She had seen more than most girls of the shabby side of life, of the perpetual tendency of want to cramp the noblest attitude. Poverty and misfortune had overhung her childhood, and she had none of the pretty delusions about life that are supposed to be the crowning grace of girlhood. This very competence, which gave her a touching reasonableness, made Glennard's situation more difficult than if he had aspired to a princess. Between them they asked so little—they knew so well how to make that little do; but they understood also, and she especially did not for a moment let him forget, that without that little the future they dreamed of was impossible.

The sight of her photograph quickened Glennard's exasperation. He was sick and ashamed of the part he was playing. He had loved her now for two years, with the tranquil tenderness that gathers depth and volume as it nears fulfilment; he knew that she would wait for him—but the certitude was an added pang. There are times when the constancy of the woman one cannot marry is almost as trying as that of the woman one does not want to.

Glennard turned up his reading-lamp and stirred the fire. He had a long evening before him, and he wanted to crowd out thought with action. He had brought some papers from his office and he spread them out on his table and squared himself to the task. . . .

It must have been an hour later that he found himself automatically fitting a key into a locked drawer. He had no more notion than a somnambulist of the mental process that had led up to this action. He was just dimly aware of having pushed aside the papers and the heavy calf volumes that a moment before had bounded his horizon, and of laying in their place, without a trace of conscious volition, the parcel he had taken from the drawer.

The letters were tied in packets of thirty or forty. There were a great many packets. On some of the envelopes the ink was fading; on others, which bore the English postmark, it was still fresh. She had been dead hardly three years, and she had written, at lengthening intervals, to the last. . . .

He undid one of the early packets—little notes written during their first acquaintance at Hillbridge. Glennard, on leaving college, had begun life in his uncle's law office in the old university town. It was there that, at the house of her father, Professor Forth, he had first met the young lady then chiefly distinguished for having, after two years of a conspicuously unhappy marriage, returned to the protection of the paternal roof.

Mrs. Aubyn was at that time an eager and somewhat tragic young woman, of complex mind and undeveloped manners, whom her crude experience of matrimony had fitted out with a stock of generalizations that exploded like bombs in the academic air of Hillbridge. In her choice of a husband she had been fortunate enough, if the paradox be permitted, to light on one so signally gifted with the faculty of putting himself in the wrong that her leaving him had the dignity of a manifesto—made her, as it were, the spokeswoman of outraged wifehood. In this light she was cherished by that dominant portion of Hillbridge society which was least indulgent to conjugal differences, and which found a proportionate pleasure in being for once able to feast openly on a dish liberally seasoned with the outrageous. So much did this endear Mrs. Aubyn to the university ladies, that they were disposed from the first to allow her more latitude of speech and action than the ill-used wife was generally accorded in Hillbridge, where misfortune was still regarded as a visitation designed to put people in their proper place and make them feel the superiority of their neighbors. The young woman so privileged combined with a kind of personal shyness an intellectual audacity that was like a deflected impulse of coquetry: one felt that if she had been prettier she would have had emotions instead of ideas. She was in fact even then what she had always remained: a genius capable of the acutest generalizations, but curiously undiscerning where her personal susceptibilities were concerned. Her psychology failed her just where it serves most women, and one felt that her brains would never be a guide to her heart. Of all this, however, Glennard thought little in the first year of their acquaintance. He was at an age when all the gifts and graces are but so much undiscriminated food to the ravening egoism of youth. In seeking Mrs. Aubyn's company he was prompted by an intuitive taste for the best as a pledge of his own superiority. The sympathy of the cleverest woman in Hillbridge was balm to his craving for distinction; it was public confirmation of his secret sense that he was cut out for a bigger place. It must not be understood that Glennard was vain. Vanity contents itself with the coarsest diet; there is no palate so fastidious as that of self-distrust. To a youth of Glennard's aspirations the encouragement of a clever woman stood for the symbol of all success. Later, when he had begun to feel his way, to gain a foothold, he would not need such support; but it served to carry him lightly and easily over what is often a period of insecurity and discouragement.

It would be unjust, however, to represent his interest in Mrs. Aubyn as a matter of calculation. It was as instinctive as love, and it missed being love by just such a hair-breadth deflection from the line of beauty as had determined the curve of Mrs. Aubyn's lips. When they met she had just published her first novel, and Glennard, who afterward had an ambitious man's impatience of distinguished women, was young enough to be dazzled by the semi-publicity it gave her. It was the kind of book that makes elderly ladies lower their voices and call each other "my dear" when they furtively discuss it; and Glennard exulted in the superior knowledge of the world that enabled him to take as a matter of course sentiments over which the university shook its head. Still more delightful was it to hear Mrs. Aubyn waken the echoes of academic drawing-rooms with audacities surpassing those of her printed page. Her intellectual independence gave a touch of comradeship to their intimacy, prolonging the illusion of college friendships based on a joyous interchange of heresies. Mrs. Aubyn and Glennard represented to each other the augur's wink behind the Hillbridge idol: they walked together in that light of young omniscience from which fate so curiously excludes one's elders.

Husbands, who are notoriously inopportune, may even die inopportunely, and this was the revenge that Mr. Aubyn, some two years after her return to Hillbridge, took upon his injured wife. He died precisely at the moment when Glennard was beginning to criticise her. It was not that she bored him; she did what was infinitely worse—she made him feel his inferiority. The sense of mental equality had been gratifying to his raw ambition; but as his self-knowledge defined itself, his understanding of her also increased; and if man is at times indirectly flattered by the moral superiority of woman, her mental ascendency is extenuated by no such oblique tribute to his powers. The attitude of looking up is a strain on the muscles; and it was becoming more and more Glennard's opinion that brains, in a woman, should be merely the obverse of beauty. To beauty Mrs. Aubyn could lay no claim; and while she had enough prettiness to exasperate him by her

incapacity to make use of it, she seemed invincibly ignorant of any of the little artifices whereby women contrive
to hide their defects and even to turn them into graces.
Her dress never seemed a part of her; all her clothes had
an impersonal air, as though they had belonged to someone else and been borrowed in an emergency that had
somehow become chronic. She was conscious enough of
her deficiencies to try to amend them by rash imitations of
the most approved models; but no woman who does not
dress well intuitively will ever do so by the light of reason,
and Mrs. Aubyn's plagiarisms, to borrow a metaphor of
her trade, somehow never seemed to be incorporated with
the text.

Genius is of small use to a woman who does not know
how to do her hair. The fame that came to Mrs. Aubyn
with her second book left Glennard's imagination untouched, or had at most the negative effect of removing
her still farther from the circle of his contracting sympathies. We are all the sport of time; and fate had so perversely ordered the chronology of Margaret Aubyn's ro-
mance that when her husband died Glennard felt as
though he had lost a friend.

It was not in his nature to be needlessly unkind; and
though he was in the impregnable position of the man who
has given a woman no more definable claim on him than
that of letting her fancy that he loves her, he would not
for the world have accentuated his advantage by any betrayal of indifference. During the first year of her widowhood their friendship dragged on with halting renewals of

sentiment, becoming more and more a banquet of empty dishes from which the covers were never removed; then Glennard went to New York to live and exchanged the faded pleasures of intercourse for the comparative novelty of correspondence. Her letters, oddly enough, seemed at first to bring her nearer than her presence. She had adopted, and she successfully maintained, a note as affectionately impersonal as his own; she wrote ardently of her work, she questioned him about his, she even bantered him on the inevitable pretty girl who was certain before long to divert the current of his confidences. To Glennard, who was almost a stranger in New York, the sight of Mrs. Aubyn's writing was like a voice of reassurance in surroundings as yet insufficiently aware of him. His vanity found a retrospective enjoyment in the sentiment his heart had rejected, and this factitious emotion drove him once or twice to Hillbridge, whence, after scenes of evasive tenderness, he returned dissatisfied with himself and her. As he made room for himself in New York and peopled the space he had cleared with the sympathies at the disposal of agreeable and self-confident young men, it seemed to him natural to infer that Mrs. Aubyn had refurnished in the same manner the void he was not unwilling his departure should have left. But in the dissolution of sentimental partnerships it is seldom that both associates are able to withdraw their funds at the same time; and Glennard gradually learned that he stood for the venture on which Mrs. Aubyn had irretrievably staked her all. It was not the kind of figure he cared to cut. He had no fancy for leaving havoc in his wake and would have preferred to sow a quick growth of oblivion in the spaces wasted by his unconsidered inroads; but if he supplied the seed, it was clearly Mrs. Aubyn's business to see to the raising of the crop. Her attitude seemed indeed to throw his own reasonableness into distincter relief; so that they might have stood for thrift and improvidence in an allegory of the affections.

It was not that Mrs. Aubyn permitted herself to be a pensioner on his bounty. He knew she had no wish to keep herself alive on the small change of sentiment; she simply fed on her own funded passion, and the luxuries it allowed her made him, even then, dimly aware that she had the secret of an inexhaustible alchemy.

Their relations remained thus negatively tender till she suddenly wrote him of her decision to go abroad to live. Her father had died, she had no near ties in Hillbridge, and London offered more scope than New York to her expanding personality. She was already famous, and her laurels were yet unharvested.

For a moment the news roused Glennard to a jealous sense of lost opportunities. He wanted, at any rate, to reassert his power before she made the final effort of escape. They had not met for over a year, but of course he could not let her sail without seeing her. She came to New York the day before her departure, and they spent its last hours together. Glennard had planned no course of action—he simply meant to let himself drift. They both drifted, for a long time, down the languid current of remi-

niscence; she seemed to sit passive, letting him push his
way back through the overgrown channels of the past. At
length she reminded him that they must bring their explorations to an end. He rose to leave, and stood looking
at her with the same uncertainty in his heart. He was tired
of her already—he was always tired of her—yet he was not
sure that he wanted her to go.

"I may never see you again," he said, as though con-
fidently appealing to her compassion.

Her look enveloped him. "And I shall see you always—always!"

"Why go then—?" escaped him.

"To be nearer you," she answered; and the words
dismissed him like a closing door.

The door was never to reopen; but through its narrow crack Glennard, as the years went on, became more
and more conscious of an inextinguishable light directing
its small ray toward the past which consumed so little of
his own commemorative oil. The reproach was taken from
this thought by Mrs. Aubyn's gradual translation into
terms of universality. In becoming a personage she so
naturally ceased to be a person that Glennard could almost
look back to his explorations of her spirit as on a visit to
some famous shrine, immortalized, but in a sense dese-
crated, by popular veneration.

Her letters from London continued to come with the
same tender punctuality; but the altered conditions of her
life, the vistas of new relationships disclosed by every
phrase, made her communications as impersonal as a piece

of journalism. It was as though the state, the world, indeed, had taken her off his hands, assuming the maintenance of a temperament that had long exhausted his slender store of reciprocity.

In the retrospective light shed by the letters he was blinded to their specific meaning. He was not a man who concerned himself with literature, and they had been to him, at first, simply the extension of her brilliant talk, later the dreaded vehicle of a tragic importunity. He knew, of course, that they were wonderful; that, unlike the authors who give their essence to the public and keep only a dry rind for their friends, Mrs. Aubyn had stored of her rarest vintage for this hidden sacrament of tenderness. Sometimes, indeed, he had been oppressed, humiliated almost, by the multiplicity of her allusions, the wide scope of her interests, her persistence in forcing her superabundance of thought and emotion into the shallow receptacle of his sympathy; but he had never thought of the letters objectively, as the production of a distinguished woman; had never measured the literary significance of her oppressive prodigality. He was almost frightened now at the wealth in his hands; the obligation of her love had never weighed on him like this gift of her imagination: it was as though he had accepted from her something to which even a reciprocal tenderness could not have justified his claim.

He sat a long time staring at the scattered pages on his desk; and in the sudden realization of what they meant he could almost fancy some alchemistic process changing them to gold as he stared.

He had the sense of not being alone in the room, of the presence of another self observing from without the stirring of sub-conscious impulses that sent flushes of humiliation to his forehead. At length he stood up, and with the gesture of a man who wishes to give outward expression to his purpose—to establish, as it were, a moral alibi—swept the letters into a heap and carried them toward the grate. But it would have taken too long to burn all the packets. He turned back to the table and one by one fitted the pages into their envelopes; then he tied up the letters and put them back into the locked drawer.

3

*I*t was one of the laws of Glennard's intercourse with
Miss Trent that he always went to see her the day after
he had resolved to give her up. There was a special charm
about the moments thus snatched from the jaws of renun-
ciation; and his sense of their significance was on this
occasion so keen that he hardly noticed the added gravity
of her welcome.

His feeling for her had become so vital a part of him
that her nearness had the quality of imperceptibly readjust-
ing his point of view, of making the jumbled phenomena
of experience fall at once into a rational perspective. In
this redistribution of values the sombre retrospect of the
previous evening shrank to a mere cloud on the edge of
consciousness. Perhaps the only service an unloved
woman can render the man she loves is to enhance and
prolong his illusions about her rival. It was the fate of
Margaret Aubyn's memory to serve as a foil to Miss

Trent's presence, and never had the poor lady thrown her successor into more vivid relief.

Miss Trent had the charm of still waters that are felt to be renewed by rapid currents. Her attention spread a tranquil surface to the demonstrations of others, and it was only in days of storm that one felt the pressure of the tides. This inscrutable composure was perhaps her chief grace in Glennard's eyes. Reserve, in some natures, implies merely the locking of empty rooms or the dissimulation of awkward encumbrances; but Miss Trent's reticence was to Glennard like the closed door to the sanctuary, and his certainty of divining the hidden treasure made him content to remain outside in the happy expectancy of the neophyte.

"You didn't come to the opera last night," she began, in the tone that seemed always rather to record a fact than to offer a reflection on it.

He answered with a discouraged gesture. "What was the use? We couldn't have talked."

"Not as well as here," she assented; adding, after a meditative pause, "As you didn't come I talked to Aunt Virginia instead."

"Ah!" he returned, the fact being hardly striking enough to detach him from the contemplation of her hands, which had fallen, as was their wont, into an attitude full of plastic possibilities. One felt them to be hands that, moving only to some purpose, were capable of intervals of serene inaction.

"We had a long talk," Miss Trent went on; and she

waited again before adding, with the increased absence of stress that marked her graver communications, "Aunt Virginia wants me to go abroad with her."

Glennard looked up with a start. "Abroad? When?"

"Now—next month. To be gone two years."

He permitted himself a movement of tender derision. "Does she really? Well, I want you to go abroad with *me*—for any number of years. Which offer do you accept?"

"Only one of them seems to require immediate consideration," she returned with a smile.

Glennard looked at her again. "You're not thinking of it?"

Her gaze dropped and she unclasped her hands. Her movements were so rare that they might have been said to italicize her words. "Aunt Virginia talked to me very seriously. It will be a great relief to mother and the others to have me provided for in that way for two years. I must think of that, you know." She glanced down at her gown, which, under a renovated surface, dated back to the first days of Glennard's wooing. "I try not to cost much—but I do."

"Good Lord!" Glennard groaned.

They sat silent till at length she gently took up the argument. "As the eldest, you know, I'm bound to consider these things. Women are such a burden. Jim does what he can for mother, but with his own children to provide for it isn't very much. You see we're all poor together."

"Your aunt isn't. She might help your mother."

"She does—in her own way."

"Exactly—that's the rich relation all over! You may be miserable in any way you like, but if you're to be happy you must be so in her way—and in her old gowns."

"I could be very happy in Aunt Virginia's old gowns," Miss Trent interposed.

"Abroad, you mean?"

"I mean wherever I felt that I was helping. And my going abroad will help."

"Of course—I see that. And I see your considerateness in putting its advantages negatively."

"Negatively?"

"In dwelling simply on what the going will take you from, not on what it will bring you to. It means a lot to a woman, of course, to get away from a life like this." He summed up in a disparaging glance the background of indigent furniture. "The question is how you'll like coming back to it."

She seemed to accept the full consequences of his thought. "I only know I don't like leaving it."

He flung back sombrely, "You don't even put it conditionally then?"

Her gaze deepened. "On what?"

He stood up and walked across the room. Then he came back and paused before her. "On the alternative of marrying me."

The slow color—even her blushes seemed deliberate—rose to her lower lids; her lips stirred, but the words resolved themselves into a smile and she waited.

He took another turn, with the thwarted step of the man whose nervous exasperation escapes through his muscles.

"And to think that in fifteen years I shall have a big practice!"

Her eyes triumphed for him. "In less!"

"The cursed irony of it! What do I care for the man I shall be then? It's slaving one's life away for a stranger!" He took her hands abruptly. "You'll go to Cannes, I suppose, or Monte Carlo? I heard Hollingsworth say to-day that he meant to take his yacht over to the Mediterranean—"

She released herself. "If you think that—"

"I don't. I almost wish I did. It would be easier, I mean." He broke off incoherently. "I believe your Aunt Virginia does, though. She somehow connotes Hollingsworth and the Mediterranean." He caught her hands again. "Alexa—if we could manage a little hole somewhere out of town?"

"Could we?" she sighed, half yielding.

"In one of those places where they make jokes about the mosquitoes," he pressed her. "Could you get on with one servant?"

"Could you get on without varnished boots?"

"Promise me you won't go, then!"

"What are you thinking of, Stephen?"

"I don't know," he stammered, the question giving unexpected form to his intention. "It's all in the air yet, of course; but I picked up a tip the other day—"

"You're not speculating?" she cried, with a kind of superstitious terror.

"Lord, no. This is a sure thing—I almost wish it wasn't; I mean if I can work it—" He had a sudden vision of the comprehensiveness of the temptation. If only he had been less sure of Dinslow! His assurance gave the situation the base element of safety.

"I don't understand you," she faltered.

"Trust me, instead!" he adjured her with sudden energy; and turning on her abruptly, "If you go, you know, you go free," he concluded.

She drew back, paling a little. "Why do you make it harder for me?"

"To make it easier for myself," he retorted.

4

The next afternoon Glennard, leaving his office earlier than usual, turned, on his way home, into one of the public libraries.

He had the place to himself at that closing hour, and the librarian was able to give an undivided attention to his tentative request for letters—collections of letters. The librarian suggested Walpole.

"I meant women—women's letters."

The librarian proffered Hannah More and Miss Martineau.

Glennard cursed his own inarticulateness. "I mean letters to—to some one person—a man; their husband—or—"

"Ah," said the inspired librarian, "Eloise and Abailard."

"Well—something a little nearer, perhaps," said Glennard, with lightness. "Didn't Mérimée—"

"The lady's letters, in that case, were not published."

"Of course not," said Glennard, vexed at his blunder.

"There are George Sand's letters to Flaubert."

"Ah!" Glennard hesitated. "Was she—were they—?" He chafed at his own ignorance of the sentimental by-paths of literature.

"If you want love-letters, perhaps some of the French eighteenth-century correspondences might suit you better—Mlle. Aïssé or Madame de Sabran—"

But Glennard insisted. "I want something modern—English or American. I want to look something up," he lamely concluded.

The librarian could only suggest George Eliot.

"Well, give me some of the French things, then—and I'll have Mérimée's letters. It was the woman who published them, wasn't it?"

He caught up his armful, transferring it, on the door-step, to a cab which carried him to his rooms. He dined alone, hurriedly, at a small restaurant near by, and returned at once to his books.

Late that night, as he undressed, he wondered what contemptible impulse had forced from him his last words to Alexa Trent. It was bad enough to interfere with the girl's chances by hanging about her to the obvious exclusion of other men, but it was worse to seem to justify his weakness by dressing up the future in delusive ambiguities. He saw himself sinking from depth to depth of sentimental cowardice in his reluctance to renounce his hold on her; and it filled him with self-disgust to think that the highest feeling of which he supposed himself capable was blent with such base elements.

His awakening was hardly cheered by the sight of her writing. He tore her note open and took in the few lines—she seldom exceeded the first page—with the lucidity of apprehension that is the forerunner of evil.

"My aunt sails on Saturday and I must give her my answer the day after tomorrow. Please don't come till then—I want to think the question over by myself. I know I ought to go. Won't you help me to be reasonable?"

It was settled, then. Well, he would help her to be reasonable; he wouldn't stand in her way; he would let her go. For two years he had been living some other, luckier man's life; the time had come when he must drop back into his own. He no longer tried to look ahead, to grope his way through the endless labyrinth of his material difficulties; a sense of dull resignation closed in on him like a fog.

"Hullo, Glennard!" a voice said, as an electric car, late that afternoon, dropped him at an uptown corner.

He looked up and met the interrogative smile of Barton Flamel, who stood on the curbstone watching the retreating car with the eye of a man philosophic enough to remember that it will be followed by another.

Glennard felt his usual impulse of pleasure at meeting Flamel; but it was not in this case curtailed by the reaction of contempt that habitually succeeded it. Probably even the few men who had known Flamel since his youth could have given no good reason for the vague mistrust that he inspired. Some people are judged by their actions, others by their ideas; and perhaps the shortest way of defining Flamel is to say that his well-known leniency of view was vaguely divined to include himself. Simple minds may have resented the discovery that his opinions were based on his perceptions; but there was certainly no more definite charge against him than that implied in the doubt as to how he would behave in an emergency, and his company was looked upon as one of those mildly unwholesome dissipations to which the prudent may occasionally yield. It now offered itself to Glennard as an easy escape from the obsession of moral problems, which somehow could no more be worn in Flamel's presence than a surplice in the street.

"Where are you going? To the club?" Flamel asked; adding, as the younger man assented, "Why not come to my studio instead? You'll see one bore instead of twenty."

The apartment which Flamel described as his studio showed, as its one claim to the designation, a perennially empty easel, the rest of its space being filled with the evidences of a comprehensive dilettanteism. Against this background, which seemed the visible expression of its owner's intellectual tolerance, rows of fine books detached themselves with a prominence showing them to be Flamel's chief care.

Glennard glanced with the eye of untrained curiosity at the lines of warm-toned morocco, while his host busied himself with the uncorking of Apollinaris.

"You've got a splendid lot of books," he said.

"They're fairly decent," the other assented, in the

curt tone of the collector who will not talk of his passion for fear of talking of nothing else; then, as Glennard, his hands in his pockets, began to stroll perfunctorily down the long line of bookcases—"Some men," Flamel irresistibly added, "think of books merely as tools, others as tooling. I'm between the two; there are days when I use them as scenery, other days when I want them as society; so that, as you see, my library represents a makeshift compromise between looks and brains, and the collectors look down on me almost as much as the students."

Glennard, without answering, was mechanically taking one book after another from the shelves. His hands slipped curiously over the smooth covers and the noiseless subsidence of opening pages. Suddenly he came on a thin volume of faded manuscript.

"What's this?" he asked with a listless sense of wonder.

"Ah, you're at my manuscript shelf. I've been going in for that sort of thing lately." Flamel came up and looked over his shoulders. "That's a bit of Stendhal—one of the Italian stories—and here are some letters of Balzac to Madame Surville."

Glennard took the book with sudden eagerness. "Who was Madame Surville?"

"His sister." He was conscious that Flamel was looking at him with the smile that was like an interrogation point. "I didn't know you cared for this kind of thing."

"I don't—at least I've never had the chance. Have you many collections of letters?"

"Lord, no—very few. I'm just beginning, and most of

the interesting ones are out of my reach. Here's a queer little collection, though—the rarest thing I've got—half a dozen of Shelley's letters to Harriet Westbrook. I had a devil of a time getting them—a lot of collectors were after them."

Glennard, taking the volume from his hand, glanced with a kind of repugnance at the interleaving of yellow crisscrossed sheets. "She was the one who drowned herself, wasn't she?"

Flamel nodded. "I suppose that little episode adds about fifty per cent. to their value," he said meditatively.

Glennard laid the book down. He wondered why he had joined Flamel. He was in no humor to be amused by the older man's talk, and a recrudescence of personal misery rose about him like an icy tide.

"I believe I must take myself off," he said. "I'd forgotten an engagement."

He turned to go; but almost at the same moment he was conscious of a duality of intention wherein his apparent wish to leave revealed itself as a last effort of the will against the overmastering desire to stay and unbosom himself to Flamel.

The older man, as though divining the conflict, laid a detaining pressure on his arm.

"Won't the engagement keep? Sit down and try one of these cigars. I don't often have the luck of seeing you here."

"I'm rather driven just now," said Glennard vaguely. He found himself seated again, and Flamel had pushed to his side a low stand holding a bottle of Apollinaris and a decanter of cognac.

Flamel, thrown back in his capacious arm-chair, surveyed him through a cloud of smoke with the comfortable tolerance of the man to whom no inconsistencies need be explained. Connivance was implicit in the air. It was the kind of atmosphere in which the outrageous loses its edge. Glennard felt a gradual relaxing of his nerves.

"I suppose one has to pay a lot for letters like that?" he heard himself asking, with a glance in the direction of the volume he had laid aside.

"Oh, so-so—depends on circumstances." Flamel viewed him thoughtfully. "Are you thinking of collecting?"

Glennard laughed. "Lord, no. The other way round."

"Selling?"

"Oh, I hardly know. I was thinking of a poor chap—"

Flamel filled the pause with a nod of interest.

"A poor chap I used to know—who died—he died last year—and who left me a lot of letters, letters he thought a great deal of—he was fond of me and left 'em to me outright, with the idea, I suppose, that they might benefit me somehow—I don't know—I'm not much up on such things—" He reached his hand to the tall glass his host had filled.

"A collection of autograph letters, eh? Any big names?"

"Oh, only one name. They're all letters written to

him—by one person, you understand; a woman, in fact—"

"Oh, a woman," said Flamel negligently.

Glennard was nettled by his obvious loss of interest. "I rather think they'd attract a good deal of notice if they were published."

Flamel still looked uninterested. "Love-letters, I suppose?"

"Oh, just—the letters a woman would write to a man she knew well. They were tremendous friends, he and she."

"And she wrote a clever letter?"

"Clever? It was Margaret Aubyn."

A great silence filled the room. It seemed to Glennard that the words had burst from him as blood gushes from a wound.

"Great Scott!" said Flamel sitting up. "A collection of Margaret Aubyn's letters? Did you say *you* had them?"

"They were left me—by my friend."

"I see. Was he—well, no matter. You're to be congratulated, at any rate. What are you going to do with them?"

Glennard stood up with a sense of weariness in all his bones. "Oh, I don't know. I haven't thought much about it. I just happened to see that some fellow was writing her life—"

"Joslin; yes. You didn't think of giving them to him?"

Glennard had lounged across the room and stood staring up at a bronze Bacchus who drooped his garlanded head above the pediment of an Italian cabinet. "What ought I to do? You're just the fellow to advise me." He felt the blood in his cheek as he spoke.

Flamel sat with meditative eye. "What do you *want* to do with them?" he asked.

"I want to publish them," said Glennard, swinging round with sudden energy—"If I can—"

"If you can? They're yours, you say?"

"They're mine fast enough. There's no one to prevent—I mean there are no restrictions—" he was arrested by the sense that these accumulated proofs of impunity might precisely stand as the strongest check on his action.

"And Mrs. Aubyn had no family, I believe?"

"No."

"Then I don't see who's to interfere," said Flamel, studying his cigar-tip.

Glennard had turned his unseeing stare on an ecstatic Saint Catherine framed in tarnished gilding.

"It's just this way," he began again, with an effort. "When letters are as personal as—as these of my friend's. . . . Well, I don't mind telling you that the cash would make a heap of difference to me; such a lot that it rather obscures my judgment—the fact is, if I could lay my hand on a few thousands now I could get into a big thing, and without appreciable risk; and I'd like to know whether you think I'd be justified—under the circumstances. . . ." He paused with a dry throat. It seemed to him at the moment that it would be impossible for him ever to sink lower in his own estimation. He was in truth less ashamed of weighing the temptation than of submitting his scruples to a man like Flamel, and affecting to appeal to sentiments of delicacy on the absence of which he had consciously reckoned. But he had reached a point where each word seemed to compel another, as each wave in a stream is forced forward by the pressure behind it; and before Flamel could speak he had faltered out—"You don't think people could say . . . could criticise the man. . . ."

"But the man's dead, isn't he?"

"He's dead—yes; but can I assume the responsibility without—"

Flamel hesitated; and almost immediately Glennard's scruples gave way to irritation. If at this hour Flamel were to affect an inopportune reluctance—!

The older man's answer reassured him. "Why need you assume any responsibility? Your name won't appear, of course; and as to your friend's, I don't see why his should either. He wasn't a celebrity himself, I suppose?"

"No, no."

"Then the letters can be addressed to Mr. Blank. Doesn't that make it all right?"

Glennard's hesitation revived. "For the public, yes. But I don't see that it alters the case for me. The question is, ought I to publish them at all?"

"Of course you ought to." Flamel spoke with invigorating emphasis. "I doubt if you'd be justified in keeping them back. Anything of Margaret Aubyn's is more or less public property by this time. She's too great for any one of us. I was only wondering how you could use them to the best advantage—to yourself, I mean. How many are there?"

"Oh, a lot; perhaps a hundred—I haven't counted. There may be more. . . ."

"Gad! What a haul! When were they written?"

"I don't know—that is—they corresponded for years. What's the odds?" He moved toward his hat with a vague impulse of flight.

"It all counts," said Flamel imperturbably. "A long correspondence—one, I mean, that covers a great deal of time—is obviously worth more than if the same number of letters had been written within a year. At any rate, you won't give them to Joslin? They'd fill a book, wouldn't they?"

"I suppose so. I don't know how much it takes to fill a book."

"Not love-letters, you say?"

"Why?" flashed from Glennard.

"Oh, nothing—only the big public is sentimental, and if they *were*—why, you could get any money for Margaret Aubyn's love-letters."

Glennard was silent.

"Are the letters interesting in themselves? I mean apart from the association with her name?"

"I'm no judge." Glennard took up his hat and thrust himself into his overcoat. "I dare say I sha'n't do anything about it. And, Flamel—you won't mention this to any one?"

"Lord, no. Well, I congratulate you. You've got a big

thing." Flamel was smiling at him from the hearth.

Glennard, on the threshold, forced a response to the smile, while he questioned with loitering indifference— "Financially, eh?"

"Rather; I should say so."

Glennard's hand lingered on the knob. "How much—should you say? You know about such things."

"Oh, I should have to see the letters; but I should say—well, if you've got enough to fill a book and they're fairly readable, and the book is brought out at the right time—say ten thousand down from the publisher, and possibly one or two more in royalties. If you got the publishers bidding against each other you might do even better; but of course I'm talking in the dark."

"Of course," said Glennard, with sudden dizziness. His hand had slipped from the knob and he stood staring down at the exotic spirals of the Persian rug beneath his feet.

"I'd have to see the letters," Flamel repeated.

"Of course—you'd have to see them. . . ." Glennard stammered; and, without turning, he flung over his shoulder an inarticulate "Good-bye. . . ."

5

*T*he little house, as Glennard strolled up to it between the trees, seemed no more than a gay tent pitched against the sunshine. It had the crispness of a freshly starched summer gown, and the geraniums on the veranda bloomed as simultaneously as the flowers in a bonnet. The garden was prospering absurdly. Seed they had sown at random—amid laughing counter-charges of incompetence—had shot up in fragrant defiance of their blunders. He smiled to see the clematis unfolding its punctual wings about the porch. The tiny lawn was smooth as a shaven cheek, and a crimson rambler mounted to the nursery window of a baby who never cried. A breeze shook the awning above the tea-table, and his wife, as he drew near, could be seen bending above a kettle that was just about to boil. So vividly did the whole scene suggest the painted bliss of a stage setting, that it would have been hardly surprising to see her step forward among the flowers and trill out her virtuous happiness from the veranda rail.

The stale heat of the long day in town, the dusty promiscuity of the suburban train, were now but the requisite foil to an evening of scented breezes and tranquil talk. They had been married more than a year, and each homecoming still reflected the freshness of their first day together. If, indeed, their happiness had a flaw, it was in resembling too closely the bright impermanence of their surroundings. Their love as yet was but the gay tent of holiday-makers.

His wife looked up with a smile. The country life suited her, and her beauty had gained depth from a stillness in which certain faces might have grown opaque.

"Are you very tired?" she asked, pouring his tea.

"Just enough to enjoy this." He rose from the chair in which he had thrown himself and bent over the tray for his cream. "You've had a visitor?" he commented, noticing a half-empty cup beside her own.

"Only Mr. Flamel," she said indifferently.

"Flamel? Again?"

She answered without show of surprise. "He left just now. His yacht is down at Laurel Bay and he borrowed a trap of the Dreshams to drive over here."

Glennard made no comment, and she went on, leaning her head back against the cushions of her bamboo seat, "He wants us to go for a sail with him next Sunday."

Glennard meditatively stirred his tea. He was trying to think of the most natural and unartificial thing to say, and his voice seemed to come from the outside, as though he were speaking behind a marionette. "Do you want to?"

"Just as you please," she said compliantly. No affectation of indifference could have been as baffling as her compliance. Glennard, of late, was beginning to feel that the surface which, a year ago, he had taken for a sheet of clear glass, might, after all, be a mirror reflecting merely his own conception of what lay behind it.

"Do you like Flamel?" he suddenly asked; to which, still engaged with her tea, she returned the feminine answer—"I thought you did."

"I do, of course," he agreed, vexed at his own incorrigible tendency to magnify Flamel's importance by hovering about the topic. "A sail would be rather jolly; let's go."

She made no reply and he drew forth the rolled-up evening papers which he had thrust into his pocket on leaving the train. As he smoothed them out his own countenance seemed to undergo the same process. He ran his eye down the list of stocks, and Flamel's importunate personality receded behind the rows of figures pushing forward into notice like so many bearers of good news. Glennard's investments were flowering like his garden: the dryest shares blossomed into dividends and a golden harvest awaited his sickle.

He glanced at his wife with the tranquil air of a man who digests good luck as naturally as the dry ground absorbs a shower. "Things are looking uncommonly well. I believe we shall be able to go to town for two or three months next winter if we can find something cheap."

She smiled luxuriously: it was pleasant to be able to

say, with an air of balancing relative advantages, "Really, on the baby's account I shall be almost sorry; but if we do go, there's Kate Erskine's house . . . she'll let us have it for almost nothing. . . ."

"Well, write her about it," he recommended, his eye travelling on in search of the weather report. He had turned to the wrong page; and suddenly a line of black characters leapt out at him as from an ambush.

MARGARET AUBYN'S LETTERS.
Two volumes. Out To-day. First Edition of five thousand sold out before leaving the press.
Second Edition ready next week. The Book of the Year. . . .

He looked up stupidly. His wife still sat with her head thrown back, her pure profile detached against the cushions. She was smiling a little over the prospect his last words had opened. Behind her head shivers of sun and shade ran across the striped awning. A row of maples and a privet hedge hid their neighbor's gables, giving them undivided possession of their leafy half-acre; and life, a moment before, had been like their plot of ground, shut off, hedged in from importunities, impenetrably his and hers. Now it seemed to him that every maple-leaf, every privet-bud, was a relentless human gaze, pressing close upon their privacy. It was as though they sat in a brightly lit room, uncurtained from a darkness full of hostile watchers. . . . His wife still smiled; and her unconsciousness of danger seemed in some horrible way to put her beyond the reach of rescue. . . .

He had not known that it would be like this. After the first odious weeks, spent in preparing the letters for publication, in submitting them to Flamel, and in negotiating with the publishers, the transaction had dropped out of his consciousness into that unvisited limbo to which we relegate the deeds we would rather not have done but have no notion of undoing. From the moment he had obtained Miss Trent's promise not to sail with her aunt he had tried to imagine himself irrevocably committed. After that, he argued, his first duty was to her—she had become his conscience. The sum obtained from the publishers by Flamel's adroit manipulations, and opportunely transferred to Dinslow's successful venture, already yielded a return which, combined with Glennard's professional earnings, took the edge of compulsion from their way of living, making it appear the expression of a graceful preference for simplicity. It was the mitigated poverty which can subscribe to a review or two and have a few flowers on the dinner-table. And already in a small way Glennard was beginning to feel the magnetic quality of prosperity. Clients who had passed his door in the hungry days sought it out now that it bore the name of a successful man. It was understood that a small inheritance, cleverly invested, was the source of his fortune; and there was a feeling that a man who could do so well for himself was likely to know how to turn over other people's money.

But it was in the more intimate reward of his wife's

happiness that Glennard tasted the full flavor of success. Coming out of conditions so narrow that those he offered her seemed spacious, she fitted into her new life without any of those manifest efforts at adjustment that are as sore to a husband's pride as the critical rearrangement of the bridal furniture. She had given him, instead, the delicate pleasure of watching her expand like a sea-creature restored to its element, stretching out the atrophied tentacles of girlish vanity and enjoyment to the rising tide of opportunity. And somehow—in the windowless inner cell of his consciousness where self-criticism cowered—Glennard's course seemed justified by its merely material success. How could such a crop of innocent blessedness have sprung from tainted soil? . . .

Now he had the injured sense of a man entrapped into a disadvantageous bargain. He had not known it would be like this; and a dull anger gathered at his heart. Anger against whom? Against his wife, for not knowing what he suffered? Against Flamel, for being the unconscious instrument of his wrongdoing? Or against that mute memory to which his own act had suddenly given a voice of accusation? Yes, that was it; and his punishment henceforth would be the presence, the unescapable presence, of the woman he had so persistently evaded. She would always be there now. It was as though he had married her instead of the other. It was what she had always wanted—to be with him—and she had gained her point at last. . . .

He sprang up, as though in an impulse of flight. . . .

The sudden movement lifted his wife's lids, and she asked, in the incurious voice of the woman whose life is enclosed in a magic circle of prosperity—"Any news?"

"No—none—" he said, roused to a sense of immediate peril. The papers lay scattered at his feet—what if she were to see them? He stretched his arm to gather them up, but his next thought showed him the futility of such concealment. The same advertisement would appear every day, for weeks to come, in every newspaper; how could he prevent her seeing it? He could not always be hiding the papers from her. . . . Well, and what if she did see it? It would signify nothing to her; the chances were that she would never even read the book. . . . As she ceased to be an element of fear in his calculations the distance between them seemed to lessen and he took her again, as it were, into the circle of his conjugal protection. . . . Yet a moment before he had almost hated her! . . . He laughed aloud at his senseless terrors. . . . He was off his balance, decidedly. . . .

"What are you laughing at?" she asked.

He explained, elaborately, that he was laughing at the recollection of an old woman in the train, an old woman with a lot of bundles, who couldn't find her ticket. . . . But somehow, in the telling, the humor of the story seemed to evaporate, and he felt the conventionality of her smile. He glanced at his watch. "Isn't it time to dress?"

She rose with serene reluctance. "It's a pity to go in. The garden looks so lovely."

They lingered side by side, surveying their domain.

There was not space in it, at this hour, for the shadow of the elm tree in the angle of the hedge: it crossed the lawn, cut the flower-border in two, and ran up the side of the house to the nursery window. She bent to flick a caterpillar from the honeysuckle; then, as they turned indoors, "If we mean to go on the yacht next Sunday," she suggested, "oughtn't you to let Mr. Flamel know?"

Glennard's exasperation deflected suddenly. "Of course I shall let him know. You always seem to imply that I'm going to do something rude to Flamel."

The words reverberated through her silence; she had a way of thus leaving one space in which to contemplate one's folly at arm's length. Glennard turned on his heel and went upstairs. As he dropped into a chair before his dressing-table, he said to himself that in the last hour he had sounded the depths of his humiliation, and that the lowest dregs of it, the very bottom-slime, was the hateful necessity of having always, as long as the two men lived, to be civil to Barton Flamel.

6

The week in town had been sultry, and the men, in the Sunday emancipation of white flannel and duck, filled the deck chairs of the yacht with their outstretched apathy, following, through a mist of cigarette smoke, the flitting inconsequences of the women. The party was a small one—Flamel had few intimate friends—but composed of more heterogeneous atoms than the little pools into which society usually runs. The reaction from the chief episode of his earlier life had bred in Glennard an uneasy distaste for any kind of personal saliency. Cleverness was useful in business; but in society it seemed to him as futile as the sham cascades formed by a stream that might have been used to drive a mill. He liked the collective point of view that goes with the civilized uniformity of dress clothes, and his wife's attitude implied the same preference; yet they found themselves slipping more and more into Flamel's intimacy. Alexa had once or twice said that she enjoyed meeting clever people; but her enjoyment took the negative form of a smiling receptivity; and Glennard felt a growing preference for the kind of people who have their thinking done for them by the community.

Still, the deck of the yacht was a pleasant refuge from the heat on shore, and his wife's profile, serenely projected against the changing blue, lay on his retina like a cool hand on the nerves. He had never been more impressed by the kind of absoluteness that lifted her beauty above the transient effects of other women, making the most harmonious face seem an accidental collocation of features.

The ladies who directly suggested this comparison were of a kind accustomed to take similar risks with more gratifying results. Mrs. Armiger had in fact long been the triumphant alternative of those who couldn't "see" Alexa Glennard's looks; and Mrs. Touchett's claims to consideration were founded on that distribution of effects which is the wonder of those who admire a highly cultivated country. The third lady of the trio which Glennard's fancy had put to such unflattering uses was bound by circumstances to support the claims of the other two. This was Mrs. Dresham, the wife of the editor of the *Radiator*. Mrs. Dresham was a lady who had rescued herself from social obscurity by assuming the rôle of her husband's exponent and interpreter; and Dresham's leisure being devoted to the cultivation of remarkable women, his wife's attitude committed her to the public celebration of their remarkableness. For the conceivable tedium of this duty, Mrs.

Dresham was repaid by the fact that there were people who took *her* for a remarkable woman; and who in turn probably purchased similar distinction with the small change of her reflected importance. As to the other ladies of the party, they were simply the wives of some of the men—the kind of women who expect to be talked to collectively and to have their questions left unanswered.

Mrs. Armiger, the latest embodiment of Dresham's instinct for the remarkable, was an innocent beauty who for years had distilled dulness among a set of people now self-condemned by their inability to appreciate her. Under Dresham's tutelage she had developed into a "thoughtful woman," who read his leaders in the *Radiator* and bought the works he recommended. When a new book appeared, people wanted to know what Mrs. Armiger thought of it; and a young gentleman who had made a trip in Touraine had recently inscribed to her the wide-margined result of his explorations.

Glennard, leaning back with his head against the rail and a slit of fugitive blue between his half-closed lids, vaguely wished she wouldn't spoil the afternoon by making people talk; though he reduced his annoyance to the minimum by not listening to what was said, there remained a latent irritation against the general futility of words.

His wife's gift of silence seemed to him the most vivid commentary on the clumsiness of speech as a means of intercourse, and his eyes had turned to her in renewed appreciation of this finer faculty when Mrs. Armiger's voice abruptly brought home to him the underrated potentialities of language.

"You've read them, of course, Mrs. Glennard?" he heard her ask; and, in reply to Alexa's vague interrogation—"Why, the *Aubyn Letters*—it's the only book people are talking of this week."

Mrs. Dresham immediately saw her advantage. "You *haven't* read them? How very extraordinary! As Mrs. Armiger says, the book's in the air: one breathes it in like the influenza."

Glennard sat motionless, watching his wife.

"Perhaps it hasn't reached the suburbs yet," she said with her unruffled smile.

"Oh, *do* let me come to you, then!" Mrs. Touchett cried; "anything for a change of air! I'm positively sick of the book and I can't put it down. Can't you sail us beyond its reach, Mr. Flamel?"

Flamel shook his head. "Not even with this breeze. Literature travels faster than steam nowadays. And the worst of it is that we can't any of us give up reading: it's as insidious as a vice and as tiresome as a virtue."

"I believe it *is* a vice, almost, to read such a book as the *Letters,*" said Mrs. Touchett. "It's the woman's soul, absolutely torn up by the roots—her whole self laid bare; and to a man who evidently didn't care; who couldn't have cared. I don't mean to read another line: it's too much like listening at a keyhole."

"But if she wanted it published?"

"Wanted it? How do we know she did?"

"Why, I heard she'd left the letters to the man—whoever he is—with directions that they should be published after his death—"

"I don't believe it," Mrs. Touchett declared.

"He's dead then, is he?" one of the men asked.

"Why, you don't suppose if he were alive he could ever hold up his head again, with these letters being read by everybody?" Mrs. Touchett protested. "It must have been horrible enough to know they'd been written to him; but to publish them! No man could have done it and no woman could have told him to—"

"Oh, come, come," Dresham judicially interposed; "after all, they're not love-letters."

"No—that's the worst of it; they're unloved letters," Mrs. Touchett retorted.

"Then, obviously, she needn't have written them; whereas the man, poor devil, could hardly help receiving them."

"Perhaps he counted on the public to save him the trouble of reading them," said young Hartly, who was in the cynical stage.

Mrs. Armiger turned her reproachful loveliness to Dresham. "From the way you defend him I believe you know who he is."

Every one looked at Dresham, and his wife smiled with the superior air of the woman who is in her husband's professional secrets. Dresham shrugged his shoulders.

"What have I said to defend him?"

"You called him a poor devil—you pitied him."

"A man who could let Margaret Aubyn write to him in that way? Of course I pity him."

"Then you *must* know who he is," cried Mrs. Armiger with a triumphant air of penetration.

Hartly and Flamel laughed and Dresham shook his head. "No one knows; not even the publishers; so they tell me at least."

"So they tell you to tell us," Hartly astutely amended; and Mrs. Armiger added, with the appearance of carrying the argument a point farther, "But even if *he's* dead and *she's* dead, somebody must have given the letters to the publishers."

"A little bird, probably," said Dresham, smiling indulgently on her deduction.

"A little bird of prey then—a vulture, I should say—" another man interpolated.

"Oh, I'm not with you there," said Dresham easily. "Those letters belonged to the public."

"How can any letters belong to the public that weren't written to the public?" Mrs. Touchett interposed.

"Well, these were, in a sense. A personality as big as Margaret Aubyn's belongs to the world. Such a mind is part of the general fund of thought. It's the penalty of greatness—one becomes a *monument historique.* Posterity pays the cost of keeping one up, but on condition that one is always open to the public."

"I don't see that that exonerates the man who gives up the keys of the sanctuary, as it were."

"Who *was* he?" another voice inquired.

"Who was he? Oh, nobody, I fancy—the letter-box, the slit in the wall through which the letters passed to posterity. . . ."

"But she never meant them for posterity!"

"A woman shouldn't write such letters if she doesn't mean them to be published. . . ."

"She shouldn't write them to such a man!" Mrs. Touchett scornfully corrected.

"I never keep letters," said Mrs. Armiger, under the obvious impression that she was contributing a valuable point to the discussion.

There was a general laugh, and Flamel, who had not spoken, said lazily, "You women are too incurably subjective. I venture to say that most men would see in those letters merely their immense literary value, their significance as documents. The personal side doesn't count where there's so much else."

"Oh, we all know you haven't any principles," Mrs. Armiger declared; and Alexa Glennard, lifting an indolent smile, said: "I shall never write you a love-letter, Mr. Flamel."

Glennard moved away impatiently. Such talk was as tedious as the buzzing of gnats. He wondered why his wife had wanted to drag him on such a senseless expedition. . . . He hated Flamel's crowd—and what business had Flamel himself to interfere in that way, standing up for the publication of the letters as though Glennard needed his defence? . . .

Glennard turned his head and saw that Flamel had

drawn a seat to Alexa's elbow and was speaking to her in a low tone. The other groups had scattered, straying in twos along the deck. It came over Glennard that he should never again be able to see Flamel speaking to his wife without the sense of sick mistrust that now loosened his joints. . . .

Alexa, the next morning, over their early breakfast, surprised her husband by an unexpected request.

"Will you bring me those letters from town?" she asked.

"What letters?" he said, putting down his cup. He felt himself as vulnerable as a man who is lunged at in the dark.

"Mrs. Aubyn's. The book they were all talking about yesterday."

Glennard, carefully measuring his second cup of tea, said with deliberation, "I didn't know you cared about that sort of thing."

She was, in fact, not a great reader, and a new book seldom reached her till it was, so to speak, on the home stretch; but she replied with a gentle tenacity, "I think it would interest me because I read her life last year."

"Her life? Where did you get that?"

"Some one lent it to me when it came out—Mr. Flamel, I think."

His first impulse was to exclaim, "Why the devil do you borrow books of Flamel? I can buy you all you want—" but he felt himself irresistibly forced into an attitude of smiling compliance. "Flamel always has the newest books going, hasn't he? You must be careful, by the way, about returning what he lends you. He's rather crotchety about his library."

"Oh, I'm always very careful," she said, with a touch of competence that struck him; and she added, as he caught up his hat: "Don't forget the letters."

Why had she asked for the book? Was her sudden wish to see it the result of some hint of Flamel's? The thought turned Glennard sick, but he preserved sufficient lucidity to tell himself, a moment later, that his last hope of self-control would be lost if he yielded to the temptation of seeing a hidden purpose in everything she said and did. How much Flamel guessed, he had no means of divining; nor could he predicate, from what he knew of the man, to what use his inferences might be put. The very qualities that had made Flamel a useful adviser made him the most dangerous of accomplices. Glennard felt himself agrope among alien forces that his own act had set in motion. . . .

Alexa was a woman of few requirements; but her wishes, even in trifles, had a definiteness that distinguished them from the fluid impulses of her kind. He knew that, having once asked for the book, she would not forget it; and he put aside, as an ineffectual expedient, his momentary idea of applying for it at the circulating library and telling her that all the copies were out. If the book was to be bought, it had better be bought at once. He left his office earlier than usual and turned in at the first bookshop on his way to the train. The show-window was stacked with conspicuously lettered volumes. *Margaret Aubyn* flashed back at him in endless iteration. He plunged into the shop and came on a counter where the name repeated itself on row after row of bindings. It seemed to have driven the rest of literature to the back shelves. He caught up a copy, tossing the money to an astonished clerk, who pursued him to the door with the unheeded offer to wrap up the volumes.

In the street he was seized with a sudden apprehension. What if he were to meet Flamel? The thought was intolerable. He called a cab and drove straight to the station, where, amid the palm-leaf fans of a perspiring crowd, he waited a long half-hour for his train to start.

He had thrust a volume in either pocket, and in the train he dared not draw them out; but the detested words leaped at him from the folds of the evening paper. The air seemed full of Margaret Aubyn's name; the motion of the train set it dancing up and down on the page of a magazine that a man in front of him was reading. . . .

At the door he was told that Mrs. Glennard was still out, and he went upstairs to his room and dragged the books from his pockets. They lay on the table before him like live things that he feared to touch. . . . At length he opened the first volume. A familiar letter sprang out at him, each word quickened by its glaring garb of type. The little broken phrases fled across the page like wounded animals in the open. . . . It was a horrible sight . . . a *battue* of helpless things driven savagely out of shelter. He had not known it would be like this. . . .

He understood now that, at the moment of selling the letters, he had viewed the transaction solely as it affected himself: as an unfortunate blemish on an otherwise presentable record. He had scarcely considered the act in relation to Margaret Aubyn; for death, if it hallows, also makes innocuous. Glennard's God was a god of the living, of the immediate, the actual, the tangible; all his days he had lived in the presence of that god, heedless of the divinities who, below the surface of our deeds and passions, silently forge the fatal weapons of the dead.

7

A knock roused him, and looking up he saw his wife. He met her glance in silence, and she faltered out, "Are you ill?"

The words restored his self-possession. "Ill? Of course not. They told me you were out and I came upstairs."

The books lay between them on the table; he wondered when she would see them. She lingered tentatively on the threshold, with the air of leaving his explanation on his hands. She was not the kind of woman who could be counted on to fortify an excuse by appearing to dispute it.

"Where have you been?" Glennard asked, moving forward so that he obstructed her vision of the books.

"I walked over to the Dreshams' for tea."

"I can't think what you see in those people," he said with a shrug; adding, uncontrollably—"I suppose Flamel was there?"

"No; he left on the yacht this morning."

An answer so obstructing to the natural escape of his irritation left Glennard with no momentary resource but that of strolling impatiently to the window. As her eyes followed him they lit on the books.

"Ah, you've brought them! I'm so glad," she said.

He answered over his shoulder, "For a woman who never reads you make the most astounding exceptions!"

Her smile was an exasperating concession to the probability that it had been hot in town or that something had bothered him.

"Do you mean it's not nice to want to read the book?" she asked. "It was not nice to publish it, certainly; but after all, I'm not responsible for that, am I?" She paused, and, as he made no answer, went on, still smiling, "I do read sometimes, you know; and I'm very fond of Margaret Aubyn's books. I was reading *Pomegranate Seed* when we first met. Don't you remember? It was then you told me all about her."

Glennard had turned back into the room and stood staring at his wife. "All about her?" he repeated, and with the words remembrance came to him. He had found Miss Trent one afternoon with the novel in her hand, and moved by the lover's fatuous impulse to associate himself in some way with whatever fills the mind of the beloved, had broken through his habitual silence about the past. Rewarded by the consciousness of figuring impressively in Miss Trent's imagination, he had gone on from one anecdote to another, reviving dormant details of his old Hillbridge life, and pasturing his vanity on the eagerness with which she listened to his reminiscences of a being already clothed in the impersonality of greatness.

The incident had left no trace in his mind; but it sprang up now like an old enemy, the more dangerous for having been forgotten. The instinct of self-preservation—sometimes the most perilous that man can exercise—made him awkwardly declare: "Oh, I used to see her at people's houses, that was all;" and her silence as usual leaving room for a multiplication of blunders, he added, with increased indifference, "I simply can't see what you can find to interest you in such a book."

She seemed to consider this intently. "You've read it, then?"

"I glanced at it—I never read such things."

"Is it true that she didn't wish the letters to be published?"

Glennard felt the sudden dizziness of the mountaineer on a narrow ledge, and with it the sense that he was lost if he looked more than a step ahead.

"I'm sure I don't know," he said; then, summoning a smile, he passed his hand through her arm. *"I* didn't have tea at the Dreshams', you know; won't you give me some now?" he suggested.

That evening Glennard, under pretext of work to be done, shut himself into the small study opening off the drawing-room. As he gathered up his papers he said to his wife: "You're not going to sit indoors on such a night as this? I'll join you presently outside."

But she had drawn her arm-chair to the lamp. "I want

to look at my book," she said, taking up the first volume of the *Letters*.

Glennard, with a shrug, withdrew into the study. "I'm going to shut the door; I want to be quiet," he explained from the threshold; and she nodded without lifting her eyes from the book.

He sank into a chair, staring aimlessly at the outspread papers. How was he to work, while on the other side of the door she sat with that volume in her hand? The door did not shut her out—he saw her distinctly, felt her close to him in a contact as painful as the pressure on a bruise.

The sensation was part of the general strangeness that made him feel like a man waking from a long sleep to find himself in an unknown country among people of alien tongue. We live in our own souls as in an unmapped region, a few acres of which we have cleared for our habitation; while of the nature of those nearest us we know but the boundaries that march with ours. Of the points in his wife's character not in direct contact with his own, Glennard now discerned his ignorance; and the baffling sense of her remoteness was intensified by the discovery that, in one way, she was closer to him than ever before. As one may live for years in happy unconsciousness of the possession of a sensitive nerve, he had lived beside his wife unaware that her individuality had become a part of the texture of his life, ineradicable as some growth on a vital organ; and he now felt himself at once incapable of forecasting her judgment and powerless to evade its effects.

To escape, the next morning, the confidences of the breakfast-table, he went to town earlier than usual. His wife, who read slowly, was given to talking over what she read, and at present his first object in life was to postpone the inevitable discussion of the letters. This instinct of protection, in the afternoon, on his way up town, guided him to the club in search of a man who might be persuaded to come out to the country to dine. The only man in the club was Flamel.

Glennard, as he heard himself almost involuntarily pressing Flamel to come and dine, felt the full irony of the situation. To use Flamel as a shield against his wife's scrutiny was only a shade less humiliating than to reckon on his wife as a defence against Flamel.

He felt a contradictory movement of annoyance at the latter's ready acceptance, and the two men drove in silence to the station. As they passed the bookstall in the waiting-room Flamel lingered a moment, and the eyes of both fell on Margaret Aubyn's name, conspicuously displayed above a counter stacked with the familiar volumes.

"We shall be late, you know," Glennard remonstrated, pulling out his watch.

"Go ahead," said Flamel imperturbably. "I want to get something—"

Glennard turned on his heel and walked down the platform. Flamel rejoined him with an innocent-looking magazine in his hand; but Glennard dared not even glance at the cover, lest it should show the syllables he feared.

The train was full of people they knew, and they were

kept apart till it dropped them at the little suburban station. As they strolled up the shaded hill, Glennard talked volubly, pointing out the improvements in the neighborhood, deploring the threatened approach of an electric railway, and screening himself by a series of reflex adjustments from the risk of any allusion to the *Letters.* Flamel suffered his discourse with the bland inattention that we accord to the affairs of some one else's suburb, and they reached the shelter of Alexa's tea-table without a perceptible turn toward the dreaded topic.

The dinner passed off safely. Flamel, always at his best in Alexa's presence, gave her the kind of attention which is like a becoming light thrown on the speaker's words: his answers seemed to bring out a latent significance in her phrases, as the sculptor draws his statue from the block. Glennard, under his wife's composure, detected a sensibility to this manoeuvre, and the discovery was like the lightning-flash across a nocturnal landscape. Thus far these momentary illuminations had served only to reveal the strangeness of the intervening country: each fresh observation seemed to increase the sum-total of his ignorance. Her simplicity of outline was more puzzling than a complex surface. One may conceivably work one's way through a labyrinth; but Alexa's candor was like a snow-covered plain, where, the road once lost, there are no landmarks to travel by.

Dinner over, they returned to the veranda, where a moon, rising behind the old elm, was combining with that complaisant tree a romantic enlargement of their borders.

Glennard had forgotten the cigars. He went to his study to fetch them, and in passing through the drawing-room he saw the second volume of the *Letters* lying open on his wife's table. He picked up the book and looked at the date of the letter she had been reading. It was one of the last . . . he knew the few lines by heart. He dropped the book and leaned against the wall. Why had he included that one among the others? Or was it possible that now they would all seem like that . . . ?

Alexa's voice came suddenly out of the dusk. "May Touchett was right—it *is* like listening at a keyhole. I wish I hadn't read it!"

Flamel returned, in the leisurely tone of the man whose phrases are punctuated by a cigarette, "It seems so to us, perhaps; but to another generation the book will be a classic."

"Then it ought not to have been published till it had time to become a classic. It's horrible, it's degrading almost, to read the secrets of a woman one might have known." She added, in a lower tone, "Stephen *did* know her—"

"Did he?" came from Flamel.

"He knew her very well, at Hillbridge, years ago. The book has made him feel dreadfully . . . he wouldn't read it . . . he didn't want me to read it. I didn't understand at first, but now I can see how horribly disloyal it must seem to him. It's so much worse to surprise a friend's secrets than a stranger's."

"Oh, Glennard's such a sensitive chap," Flamel said

easily; and Alexa almost rebukingly rejoined, "If you'd known her I'm sure you'd feel as he does. . . ."

Glennard stood motionless, overcome by the singular infelicity with which he had contrived to put Flamel in possession of the two points most damaging to his case: the fact that he had been a friend of Margaret Aubyn's and that he had concealed from Alexa his share in the publication of the letters. To a man of less than Flamel's astuteness it must now be clear to whom the letters were addressed; and the possibility once suggested, nothing could be easier than to confirm it by discreet research. An impulse of self-accusal drove Glennard to the window. Why not anticipate betrayal by telling his wife the truth in Flamel's presence? If the man had a drop of decent feeling in him, such a course would be the surest means of securing his silence; and above all, it would rid Glennard of the necessity of defending himself against the perpetual criticism of his wife's belief in him. . . .

The impulse was strong enough to carry him to the window; but there a reaction of defiance set in. What had he done, after all, to need defence and explanation? Both Dresham and Flamel had, in his hearing, declared the publication of the letters to be not only justifiable but obligatory; and if the disinterestedness of Flamel's verdict might be questioned, Dresham's at least represented the impartial view of the man of letters. As to Alexa's words, they were simply the conventional utterance of the "nice" woman on a question already decided for her by other "nice" women. She had said the proper thing as mechanically as she would have put on the appropriate gown or written the correct form of dinner invitation. Glennard had small faith in the abstract judgments of the other sex: he knew that half the women who were horrified by the publication of Mrs. Aubyn's letters would have betrayed her secrets without a scruple.

The sudden lowering of his emotional pitch brought a proportionate relief. He told himself that now the worst was over and things would fall into perspective again. His wife and Flamel had turned to other topics, and coming out on the veranda, he handed the cigars to Flamel, saying cheerfully—and yet he could have sworn they were the last words he meant to utter!—"Look here, old man, before you go down to Newport you must come out and spend a few days with us—mustn't he, Alexa?"

8

Glennard, perhaps unconsciously, had counted on the continuance of this easier mood. He had always taken pride in a certain robustness of fibre that enabled him to harden himself against the inevitable, to convert his failures into the building materials of success. Though it did not even now occur to him that what he called the inevitable had hitherto been the alternative he happened to prefer, he was yet obscurely aware that his present difficulty was one not to be conjured by any affectation of indifference. Some griefs build the soul a spacious house, but in this misery of Glennard's he could not stand upright. It pressed against him at every turn. He told himself that this was because there was no escape from the visible evidences of his act. The *Letters* confronted him everywhere. People who had never opened a book discussed them with critical reservations; to have read them had become a social obligation in circles to which literature never penetrates except in a personal guise.

Glennard did himself injustice. It was from the unexpected discovery of his own pettiness that he chiefly suffered. Our self-esteem is apt to be based on the hypothetical great act we have never had occasion to perform; and even the most self-scrutinizing modesty credits itself negatively with a high standard of conduct. Glennard had never thought himself a hero; but he had been certain that he was incapable of baseness. We all like our wrongdoings to have a becoming cut, to be made to order, as it were; and Glennard found himself suddenly thrust into a garb of dishonor surely meant for a meaner figure.

The immediate result of his first weeks of wretchedness was the resolve to go to town for the winter. He knew that such a course was just beyond the limit of prudence; but it was easy to allay the fears of Alexa, who, scrupulously vigilant in the management of the household, preserved the American wife's usual aloofness from her husband's business cares. Glennard felt that he could not trust himself to a winter's solitude with her. He had an unspeakable dread of her learning the truth about the letters, yet could not be sure of steeling himself against the suicidal impulse of avowal. His very soul was parched for sympathy; he thirsted for a voice of pity and comprehension. But would his wife pity? Would she understand? Again he found himself brought up abruptly against his incredible ignorance of her nature. The fact that he knew well enough how she would behave in the ordinary emergencies of life, that he could count, in such contingencies, on the kind of high courage and directness he had always divined in her, made him the more hopeless of her entering into the tortuous psychology of an act that he himself could no longer explain or understand. It would have been easier had she been more complex, more feminine— if he could have counted on her imaginative sympathy or her moral obtuseness—but he was sure of neither. He was sure of nothing but that, for a time, he must avoid her. Glennard could not rid himself of the delusion that by and by his action would cease to make its consequences felt. He would not have cared to own to himself that he counted on the dulling of his sensibilities: he preferred to indulge the vague hypothesis that extraneous circumstances would somehow efface the blot upon his conscience. In his worst moments of self-abasement he tried to find solace in the thought that Flamel had sanctioned his course. Flamel, at the outset, must have guessed to whom the letters were addressed; yet neither then nor afterward had he hesitated to advise their publication. This thought drew Glennard to him in fitful impulses of friendliness, from each of which there was a sharper reaction of distrust and aversion. When Flamel was not at the house, he missed the support of his tacit connivance; when he was there, his presence seemed the assertion of an intolerable claim.

Early in the winter the Glennards took possession of the little house that was to cost them almost nothing. The change brought Glennard the relief of seeing less of his wife, and of being protected, in her presence, by the multiplied preoccupations of town life. Alexa, who could never appear hurried, showed the smiling abstraction of a pretty woman to whom the social side of married life has not lost its novelty. Glennard, with the recklessness of a man fresh from his first financial imprudence, encouraged her in such little extravagances as her good sense at first resisted. Since they had come to town, he argued, they might as well enjoy themselves. He took a sympathetic view of the necessity of new gowns, he gave her a set of furs at Christmas, and before the New Year they had agreed on the necessity of adding a parlor-maid to their small establishment.

Providence the very next day hastened to justify this measure by placing on Glennard's breakfast-plate an envelope bearing the name of the publishers to whom he had sold Mrs. Aubyn's letters. It happened to be the only letter the early post had brought, and he glanced across the table at his wife, who had come down before him and had probably laid the envelope on his plate. She was not the woman to ask awkward questions, but he felt the conjecture of her glance, and he was debating whether to affect surprise at the receipt of the letter, or to pass it off as a business communication that had strayed to his house, when a check fell from the envelope. It was the royalty on the first edition of the letters. His first feeling was one of simple satisfaction. The money had come with such infernal opportuneness that he could not help welcoming it. Before long, too, there would be more; he knew the book was still selling far beyond the publishers' previsions. He put the check in his pocket and left the room without looking at his wife.

On the way to his office the habitual reaction set in. The money he had received was the first tangible reminder that he was living on the sale of his self-esteem. The thought of material benefit had been overshadowed by his sense of the intrinsic baseness of making the letters known: now he saw what an element of sordidness it added to the situation and how the fact that he needed the money, and must use it, pledged him more irrevocably than ever to the consequences of his act. It seemed to him, in that first hour of misery, that he had betrayed his friend anew.

When, that afternoon, he reached home earlier than usual, Alexa's drawing-room was full of a gayety that overflowed to the stairs. Flamel, for a wonder, was not there; but Dresham and young Hartly, grouped about the tea-table, were receiving with resonant mirth a narrative delivered in the fluttered staccato that made Mrs. Armiger's conversation like the ejaculations of a startled aviary.

She paused as Glennard entered, and he had time to notice that his wife, who was busied about the tea-tray, had not joined in the laughter of the men.

"Oh, go on, go on," young Hartly rapturously groaned; and Mrs. Armiger met Glennard's inquiry with the deprecating cry that really she didn't see what there was to laugh at. "I'm sure I feel more like crying. I don't know what I should have done if Alexa hadn't been at

home to give me a cup of tea. My nerves are in shreds—
yes, another, dear, please—" and as Glennard looked his
perplexity, she went on, after pondering on the selection
of a second lump of sugar, "Why, I've just come from the
reading, you know—the reading at the Waldorf."

"I haven't been in town long enough to know anything," said Glennard, taking the cup his wife handed him.
"Who has been reading what?"

"That lovely girl from the South—Georgie—Georgie. What's-her-name—Mrs. Dresham's protégée—unless
she's *yours,* Mr. Dresham! Why, the big ball-room was
packed, and all the women were crying like idiots—it was
the most harrowing thing I ever heard—"

"What *did* you hear?" Glennard asked; and his wife
interposed: "Won't you have another bit of cake, Julia?
Or, Stephen, ring for some hot toast, please." Her tone
betrayed a polite weariness of the topic under discussion.
Glennard turned to the bell, but Mrs. Armiger pursued
him with her lovely amazement.

"Why, the *Aubyn Letters*—didn't you know about it?
She read them so beautifully that it was quite horrible—I
should have fainted if there'd been a man near enough to
carry me out."

Hartly's glee redoubled, and Dresham said jovially,
"How like you women to raise a shriek over the book and
then do all you can to encourage the blatant publicity of
the readings!"

Mrs. Armiger met him more than half-way on a tor-
rent of self-accusal. "It *was* horrid; it was disgraceful. I told

your wife we ought all to be ashamed of ourselves for going, and I think Alexa was quite right to refuse to take any tickets—even if it was for a charity."

"Oh," her hostess murmured indifferently, "with me charity begins at home. I can't afford emotional luxuries."

"A charity? A charity?" Hartly exulted. "I hadn't seized the full beauty of it. Reading poor Margaret Aubyn's love-letters at the Waldorf before five hundred people for a charity! *What* charity, dear Mrs. Armiger?"

"Why, the Home for Friendless Women—"

"It was well chosen," Dresham commented; and Hartly buried his mirth in the sofa cushions.

When they were alone Glennard, still holding his untouched cup of tea, turned to his wife, who sat silently behind the kettle. "Who asked you to take a ticket for that reading?"

"I don't know, really—Kate Dresham, I fancy. It was she who got it up."

"It's just the sort of damnable vulgarity she's capable of! It's loathsome—it's monstrous—"

His wife, without looking up, answered gravely, "I thought so too. It was for that reason I didn't go. But you must remember that very few people feel about Mrs. Aubyn as you do—"

Glennard managed to set down his cup with a steady hand, but the room swung round with him and he dropped into the nearest chair. "As I do?" he repeated.

"I mean that very few people knew her when she

lived in New York. To most of the women who went to the reading she was a mere name, too remote to have any personality. With me, of course, it was different—"

Glennard gave her a startled look. "Different? Why different?"

"Since you were her friend—"

"Her friend!" He stood up. "You speak as if she had had only one—the most famous woman of her day!" He moved vaguely about the room, bending down to look at some books on the table. "I hope," he added, "you didn't give that as a reason?"

"A reason?"

"For not going. A woman who gives reasons for getting out of social obligations is sure to make herself unpopular or ridiculous."

The words were uncalculated; but in an instant he saw that they had strangely bridged the distance between his wife and himself. He felt her close on him, like a panting foe; and her answer was a flash that showed the hand on the trigger.

"I seem," she said from the threshold, "to have done both in giving my reason to you."

The fact that they were dining out that evening made it easy for him to avoid Alexa till she came downstairs in her opera-cloak. Mrs. Touchett, who was going to the same dinner, had offered to call for her; and Glennard, refusing a precarious seat between the ladies' draperies, followed on foot. The evening was interminable. The reading at the Waldorf, at which all the women had been present, had revived the discussion of the *Aubyn Letters,* and Glennard, hearing his wife questioned as to her absence, felt himself miserably wishing that she had gone, rather than that her staying away should have been remarked. He was rapidly losing all sense of proportion where the *Letters* were concerned. He could no longer hear them mentioned without suspecting a purpose in the allusion; he even yielded himself for a moment to the extravagance of imagining that Mrs. Dresham, whom he disliked, had organized the reading in the hope of making him betray himself—for he was already sure that Dresham had divined his share in the transaction.

The attempt to keep a smooth surface on this inner tumult was as endless and unavailing as efforts made in a nightmare. He lost all sense of what he was saying to his neighbors; and once when he looked up his wife's glance struck him cold.

She sat nearly opposite him, at Flamel's side, and it appeared to Glennard that they had built about themselves one of those airy barriers of talk behind which two people can say what they please. While the reading was discussed they were silent. Their silence seemed to Glennard almost cynical—it stripped the last disguise from their complicity. A throb of anger rose in him, but suddenly it fell, and he felt, with a curious sense of relief, that at bottom he no longer cared whether Flamel had told his wife or not. The assumption that Flamel knew about the letters had become a fact to Glennard; and it now seemed to him better that Alexa should know too.

He was frightened at first by the discovery of his own

indifference. The last barriers of his will seemed to be breaking down before a flood of moral lassitude. How could he continue to play his part, how keep his front to the enemy, with this poison of indifference stealing through his veins? He tried to brace himself with the remembrance of his wife's scorn. He had not forgotten the note on which their conversation had closed. If he had ever wondered how she would receive the truth he wondered no longer—she would despise him. But this lent a new insidiousness to his temptation, since her contempt would be a refuge from his own. He said to himself that, since he no longer cared for the consequences, he could at least acquit himself of speaking in self-defence. What he wanted now was not immunity but castigation: his wife's indignation might still reconcile him to himself. Therein lay his one hope of regeneration; her scorn was the moral antiseptic that he needed, her comprehension the one balm that could heal him. . . .

When they left the dinner he was so afraid of speaking that he let her drive home alone, and went to the club with Flamel.

9

*H*e rose next morning with the resolve to know what Alexa thought of him. It was not anchoring in a haven but lying to in a storm—he felt the need of a temporary lull in the turmoil of his sensations.

He came home late, for they were dining alone and he knew that they would have the evening together. When he followed her to the drawing-room after dinner he thought himself on the point of speaking; but as she handed him his coffee he said involuntarily: "I shall have to carry this off to the study; I've got a lot of work tonight."

Alone in the study he cursed his cowardice. What was it that had withheld him? A certain bright unapproachableness seemed to keep him at arm's length. She was not the kind of woman whose compassion could be circumvented; there was no chance of slipping past the outposts—he would never take her by surprise. Well—why not face her, then? What he shrank from could be no worse than what he was enduring. He had pushed back his chair and turned to go upstairs when a new expedient presented itself. What if, instead of telling her, he were to let her find out for herself and watch the effect of the discovery before speaking? In this way he made over to chance the burden of the revelation.

The idea had been suggested by the sight of the formula enclosing the publisher's check. He had deposited the money, but the notice accompanying it dropped from his note-case as he cleared his table for work. It was the formula usual in such cases, and revealed clearly enough that he was the recipient of a royalty on Margaret Aubyn's letters. It would be impossible for Alexa to read it without understanding at once that the letters had been written to him and that he had sold them. . . .

He sat downstairs till he heard her ring for the parlor-maid to put out the lights; then he went up to the drawing-room with a bundle of papers in his hand. Alexa was just rising from her seat, and the lamplight fell on the deep roll of hair that overhung her brow like the eaves of a temple. Her face had often the high secluded look of a shrine; and it was this touch of awe in her beauty that now made him feel himself on the brink of sacrilege.

Lest the feeling should control him, he spoke at once. "I've brought you a piece of work—a lot of old bills and things that I want you to sort for me. Some are not worth keeping—but you'll be able to judge of that. There may be a letter or two among them—nothing of much account;

but I don't like to throw away the whole lot without having them looked over, and I haven't time to do it myself."

He held out the papers, and she took them with a smile that seemed to recognize in the service he asked the tacit intention of making amends for the incident of the previous day.

"Are you sure I shall know which to keep?"

"Oh, quite sure," he answered easily; "and besides, none are of much importance."

The next morning he invented an excuse for leaving the house without seeing her, and when he returned, just before dinner, he found a visitor's hat and stick in the hall. The visitor was Flamel, who was just taking leave.

He had risen, but Alexa remained seated; and their attitude gave the impression of a colloquy that had prolonged itself beyond the limits of speech. Both turned a surprised eye on Glennard, and he had the sense of walking into a room grown suddenly empty, as though their thoughts were conspirators dispersed by his approach. He felt the clutch of his old fear. What if his wife had already sorted the papers and had told Flamel of her discovery? Well, it was no news to Flamel that Glennard was in receipt of a royalty on the *Aubyn Letters* . . .

A sudden resolve to know the worst made him lift his eyes to his wife as the door closed on Flamel. But Alexa had risen also, and bending over her writing-table, with her back to Glennard, was beginning to speak precipitately.

"I'm dining out to-night—you don't mind my deserting you? Julia Armiger sent me word just now that she had an extra ticket for the last Ambrose concert. She told me to say how sorry she was that she hadn't two, but I knew *you* wouldn't be sorry!" She ended with a laugh that had the effect of being a strayed echo of Mrs. Armiger's; and before Glennard could speak she had added, with her hand on the door, "Mr. Flamel stayed so late that I've hardly time to dress. The concert begins ridiculously early, and Julia dines at half-past seven."

Glennard stood alone in the empty room that seemed somehow full of an ironical consciousness of what was happening. "She hates me," he murmured. "She hates me . . ."

The next day was Sunday, and Glennard purposely lingered late in his room. When he came downstairs his wife was already seated at the breakfast-table. She lifted her usual smile to his entrance and they took shelter in the nearest topic, like wayfarers overtaken by a storm. While he listened to her account of the concert he began to think that, after all, she had not yet sorted the papers, and that her agitation of the previous day must be ascribed to another cause, in which perhaps he had but an indirect concern. He wondered it had never before occurred to him that Flamel was the kind of man who might very well please a woman at his own expense, without need of fortuitous assistance. If this possibility cleared the outlook it did not brighten it. Glennard merely felt himself left alone with his baseness.

Alexa left the breakfast-table before him, and when he went up to the drawing-room he found her dressed to go out.

"Aren't you a little early for church?" he asked.

She replied that, on the way there, she meant to stop a moment at her mother's; and while she drew on her gloves he fumbled among the knick-knacks on the mantel-piece for a match to light his cigarette.

"Well, good-bye," she said, turning to go; and from the threshold she added: "By the way, I've sorted the papers you gave me. Those that I thought you would like to keep are on your study table." She went downstairs and he heard the door close behind her.

She had sorted the papers—she knew, then—she *must* know—and she had made no sign!

Glennard, he hardly knew how, found himself once more in the study. On the table lay the packet he had given her. It was much smaller—she had evidently gone over the papers with care, destroying the greater number. He loos-ened the elastic band and spread the remaining envelopes on his desk. The publisher's notice was among them.

10

*H*is wife knew and she made no sign. Glennard found himself in the case of the seafarer who, closing his eyes at nightfall on a scene he thinks to put leagues behind him before day, wakes to a port-hole framing the same patch of shore. From the kind of exaltation to which his resolve had lifted him he dropped to an unreasoning apathy. His impulse of confession had acted as a drug to self-reproach. He had tried to shift a portion of his burden to his wife's shoulders; and now that she had tacitly refused to carry it, he felt the load too heavy to be taken up.

A fortunate interval of hard work brought respite from this phase of sterile misery. He went West to argue an important case, won it, and came back to fresh preoccupations. His own affairs were thriving enough to engross him in the pauses of his professional work, and for over two months he had little time to look himself in the face. Not unnaturally—for he was as yet unskilled in the subtleties of introspection—he mistook his temporary insensibility for a gradual revival of moral health.

He told himself that he was recovering his sense of proportion, getting to see things in their true light; and if he now thought of his rash appeal to his wife's sympathy it was as an act of folly from the consequences of which he had been saved by the providence that watches over madmen. He had little leisure to observe Alexa; but he concluded that the common sense momentarily denied him had counselled her silent acceptance of the inevitable. If such a quality was a poor substitute for the passionate justness that had once seemed to distinguish her, he accepted the alternative as a part of that general lowering of the key that seems needful to the maintenance of the matrimonial duet. What woman ever retained her abstract sense of justice where another woman was concerned? Possibly the thought that he had profited by Mrs. Aubyn's tenderness was not wholly disagreeable to his wife.

When the pressure of work began to lessen, and he found himself, in the lengthening afternoons, able to reach home somewhat earlier, he noticed that the little drawing-room was always full and that he and his wife seldom had an evening alone together. When he was tired, as often happened, she went out alone; the idea of giving up an engagement to remain with him seemed not to occur to her. She had shown, as a girl, little fondness for society, nor had she seemed to regret it during the year they had spent in the country. He reflected, however, that

he was sharing the common lot of husbands, who proverbially mistake the early ardors of housekeeping for a sign
of settled domesticity. Alexa, at any rate, was refuting his
theory as inconsiderately as a seedling defeats the gar-
dener's expectations. An undefinable change had come
over her. In one sense it was a happy one, since she had
grown, if not handsomer, at least more vivid and expressive; her beauty had become more communicable: it was
as though she had learned the conscious exercise of intuitive attributes and now used her effects with the discrimi-
nation of an artist skilled in values. To a dispassionate critic
(as Glennard now rated himself) the art may at times have
been a little too obvious. Her attempts at lightness lacked
spontaneity, and she sometimes rasped him by laughing
like Julia Armiger; but he had enough imagination to
perceive that, in respect of his wife's social arts, a husband
necessarily sees the wrong side of the tapestry.

In this ironical estimate of their relation Glennard
found himself strangely relieved of all concern as to his
wife's feelings for Flamel. From an Olympian pinnacle of
indifference he calmly surveyed their inoffensive antics. It
was surprising how his cheapening of his wife put him at
ease with himself. Far as he and she were from each other
they yet had, in a sense, the tacit nearness of complicity.
Yes, they were accomplices; he could no more be jealous
of her than she could despise him. The jealousy that would
once have seemed a blur on her whiteness now appeared
like a tribute to ideals in which he no longer believed.

Glennard was little given to exploring the outskirts of literature. He always skipped the "literary notices" in the papers, and he had small leisure for the intermittent pleasures of the periodical. He had therefore no notion of the prolonged reverberations which the *Aubyn Letters* had awakened. When the book ceased to be talked about he supposed it had ceased to be read; and this apparent subsidence of the agitation about it brought the reassuring sense that he had exaggerated its vitality. The conviction, if it did not ease his conscience, at least offered him the relative relief of obscurity; he felt like an offender taken down from the pillory and thrust into the soothing darkness of a cell.

But one evening, when Alexa had left him to go to a dance, he chanced to turn over the magazines on her table, and the copy of the *Horoscope* to which he settled down with his cigar confronted him, on its first page, with a portrait of Margaret Aubyn. It was a reproduction of the photograph that had stood so long on his desk. The desiccating air of memory had turned her into the mere abstraction of a woman, and this unexpected evocation seemed to bring her nearer than she had ever been in life. Was it because he understood her better? He looked long into her eyes; little personal traits reached out to him like caresses—the tired droop of her lids, her quick way of leaning forward as she spoke, the movements of her long expressive hands. All that was feminine in her, the quality he had always missed, stole toward him from her unreproachful gaze; and now that it was too late, life had developed in him the subtler perceptions which could detect it in even this poor semblance of herself. For a moment he found consolation in the thought that, at any cost, they had thus been brought together; then a sense of shame rushed over him. Face to face with her, he felt himself laid bare to the inmost fold of consciousness. The shame was deep, but it was a renovating anguish: he was like a man whom intolerable pain has roused from the creeping lethargy of death . . .

He rose next morning to as fresh a sense of life as though his hour of communion with Margaret Aubyn had been a more exquisite renewal of their earlier meetings. His waking thought was that he must see her again; and as consciousness affirmed itself he felt an intense fear of losing the sense of her nearness. But she was still close to him: her presence remained the one reality in a world of shadows. All through his working hours he was reliving with incredible minuteness every incident of their obliterated past: as a man who has mastered the spirit of a foreign tongue turns with renewed wonder to the pages his youth has plodded over. In this lucidity of retrospection the most trivial detail had its meaning, and the joy of recovery was embittered to Glennard by the perception of all that he had missed. He had been pitiably, grotesquely stupid; and there was irony in the thought that, but for the crisis through which he was passing, he might have lived on in complacent ignorance of his loss. It was as though she had bought him with her blood . . .

That evening he and Alexa dined alone. After dinner he followed her to the drawing-room. He no longer felt the need of avoiding her; he was hardly conscious of her presence. After a few words they lapsed into silence, and he sat smoking with his eyes on the fire. It was not that he was unwilling to talk to her; he felt a curious desire to be as kind as possible; but he was always forgetting that she was there. Her full bright presence, through which the currents of life flowed so warmly, had grown as tenuous as a shadow, and he saw so far beyond her.

Presently she rose and began to move about the room. She seemed to be looking for something, and he roused himself to ask what she wanted.

"Only the last number of the *Horoscope.* I thought I'd left it on this table." He said nothing, and she went on: "You haven't seen it?"

"No," he returned coldly. The magazine was locked in his desk.

His wife had moved to the mantelpiece. She stood facing him, and as he looked up he met her tentative gaze. "I was reading an article in it—a review of Mrs. Aubyn's *Letters,*" she added slowly, with her deep deliberate blush.

Glennard stooped to toss his cigar into the fire. He felt a savage wish that she would not speak the other woman's name; nothing else seemed to matter.

"You seem to do a lot of reading," he said.

She still confronted him. "I was keeping this for you—I thought it might interest you," she said with an air of gentle insistence.

He stood up and turned away. He was sure she knew
that he had taken the review, and he felt that he was
beginning to hate her again.

"I haven't time for such things," he said indifferently.
As he moved to the door he heard her take a hurried step
forward; then she paused, and sank without speaking into
the chair from which he had risen.

11

*A*s Glennard, in the raw February sunlight, mounted the road to the cemetery, he felt the beatitude that comes with an abrupt cessation of physical pain. He had reached the point where self-analysis ceases; the impulse that moved him was purely intuitive. He did not even seek a reason for it, beyond the obvious one that his desire to stand by Margaret Aubyn's grave was prompted by no attempt at a sentimental reparation, but rather by the need to affirm in some way the reality of the tie between them.

The ironical promiscuity of death had brought Mrs. Aubyn back to share the hospitality of her husband's last lodging; but though Glennard knew she had been buried near New York he had never visited her grave. He was oppressed, as he now threaded the long avenues, by a chilling vision of her return. There was no family to follow her hearse; she had died alone, as she had lived; and the "distinguished mourners" who had formed the escort of the famous writer knew nothing of the woman they were committing to the grave. Glennard could not even remember at what season she had been buried; but his mood indulged the fancy that it must have been on some such day of harsh sunlight, the incisive February brightness that gives perspicuity without warmth. The white avenues stretched before him interminably, lined with stereotyped emblems of affliction, as though all the platitudes ever uttered had been turned to marble and set up over the unresisting dead. Here and there, no doubt, a frigid urn or an insipid angel imprisoned some fine-fibred grief, as the most hackneyed words may become the vehicle of rare meanings; but for the most part the endless alignment of monuments seemed to embody those easy generalizations about death that do not disturb the repose of the living. Glennard's eye, as he followed the way pointed out to him, had instinctively sought some low mound with a quiet headstone. He had forgotten that the dead seldom plan their own houses, and with a pang he discovered the name he sought on the cyclopean base of a shaft rearing its aggressive height at the angle of two avenues.

"How she would have hated it!" he murmured.

A bench stood near and he seated himself. The monument rose before him like some pretentious uninhabited dwelling: he could not believe that Margaret Aubyn lay there. It was a Sunday morning, and black figures moved among the paths, placing flowers on the frost-bound hillocks. Glennard noticed that the neighboring graves had been thus newly dressed, and he fancied a blind stir of expectancy through the sod, as though the bare mounds spread a parched surface to that commemorative rain. He rose presently and walked back to the entrance of the cemetery. Several greenhouses stood near the gates, and turning in at the first he asked for some flowers.

"Anything in the emblematic line?" asked the anæmic man behind the dripping counter.

Glennard shook his head.

"Just cut flowers? This way then." The florist unlocked a glass door and led him down a moist green aisle. The hot air was choked with the scent of white azaleas, white lilies, white lilacs; all the flowers were white: they were like a prolongation, a mystic efflorescence, of the long rows of marble tombstones, and their perfume seemed to cover an odor of decay. The rich atmosphere made Glennard dizzy. As he leaned in the doorway, waiting for the flowers, he had a penetrating sense of Margaret Aubyn's nearness—not the imponderable presence of his inner vision, but a life that beat warm in his arms . . .

The sharp air caught him as he stepped out into it again. He walked back and scattered the flowers over the grave. The edges of the white petals shrivelled like burnt paper in the cold; and as he watched them the illusion of her nearness faded, shrank back frozen.

12

The motive of his visit to the cemetery remained undefined save as a final effort of escape from his wife's inexpressive acceptance of his shame. It seemed to him that as long as he could keep himself alive to that shame he would not wholly have succumbed to its consequences. His chief fear was that he should become the creature of his act. His wife's indifference degraded him: it seemed to put him on a level with his dishonor. Margaret Aubyn would have abhorred the deed in proportion to her pity for the man. The sense of her potential pity drew him back to her. The one woman knew but did not understand; the other, it sometimes seemed, understood without knowing.

In its last disguise of retrospective remorse, his self-pity affected a desire for solitude and meditation. He lost himself in morbid musings, in futile visions of what life with Margaret Aubyn might have been. There were moments when, in the strange dislocation of his view, the wrong he had done her seemed a tie between them.

To indulge these emotions he fell into the habit, on Sunday afternoons, of solitary walks prolonged till after dusk. The days were lengthening, there was a touch of spring in the air, and his wanderings now usually led him to the Park and its outlying regions.

One Sunday, tired of aimless locomotion, he took a cab at the Park gates and let it carry him out to the Riverside Drive. It was a gray afternoon streaked with east wind. Glennard's cab advanced slowly, and as he leaned back, gazing with absent intentness at the deserted paths that wound under bare boughs between grass banks of premature vividness, his attention was arrested by two figures walking ahead of him. This couple, who had the path to themselves, moved at an uneven pace, as though adapting their gait to a conversation marked by meditative intervals. Now and then they paused, and in one of these pauses the lady, turning toward her companion, showed Glennard the outline of his wife's profile. The man was Flamel.

The blood rushed to Glennard's forehead. He sat up with a jerk and pushed back the lid in the roof of the hansom; but when the cabman bent down he dropped into his seat without speaking. Then, becoming conscious of the prolonged interrogation of the lifted lid, he called out—"Turn—drive back—anywhere—I'm in a hurry—"

As the cab swung round he caught a last glimpse of the two figures. They had not moved; Alexa, with bent head, stood listening.

"My God, my God—" he groaned.

It was hideous—it was abominable—he could not understand it. The woman was nothing to him—less than nothing—yet the blood hummed in his ears and hung a cloud before him. He knew it was only the stirring of the primal instinct, that it had no more to do with his reasoning self than any reflex impulse of the body; but that merely lowered anguish to disgust. Yes, it was disgust he felt—almost a physical nausea. The poisonous fumes of life were in his lungs. He was sick, unutterably sick . . .

He drove home and went to his room. They were giving a little dinner that night, and when he came down the guests were arriving. He looked at his wife: her beauty was extraordinary, but it seemed to him the beauty of a smooth sea along an unlit coast. She frightened him.

He sat late in his study. He heard the parlormaid lock the front door; then his wife went upstairs and the lights were put out. His brain was like some great empty hall with an echo in it: one thought reverberated endlessly . . . At length he drew his chair to the table and began to write. He addressed an envelope and then slowly re-read what he had written.

My dear Flamel,

Many apologies for not sending you sooner the enclosed check, which represents the customary percentage of the sale of the "Letters."

Trusting you will excuse the oversight,

Yours truly

Stephen Glennard.

139

He let himself out of the darkened house and dropped the letter in the post-box at the corner.

The next afternoon he was detained late at his office, and as he was preparing to leave he heard some one asking for him in the outer room. He seated himself again and Flamel was shown in.

The two men, as Glennard pushed aside an obstructive chair, had a moment to measure each other; then Flamel advanced, and drawing out his note-case, laid a slip of paper on the desk.

"My dear fellow, what on earth does this mean?"

Glennard recognized his check.

"That I was remiss, simply. It ought to have gone to you before."

Flamel's tone had been that of unaffected surprise, but at this his accent changed and he asked quickly: "On what ground?"

Glennard had moved away from the desk and stood leaning against the calf-backed volumes of the bookcase. "On the ground that you sold Mrs. Aubyn's letters for me, and that I find the intermediary in such cases is entitled to a percentage on the sale."

Flamel paused before answering. "You find, you say. It's a recent discovery?"

"Obviously, from my not sending the check sooner. You see I'm new to the business."

"And since when have you discovered that there was any question of business, as far as I was concerned?"

Glennard flushed and his voice rose slightly. "Are

you reproaching me for not having remembered it sooner?"

Flamel, who had spoken in the rapid repressed tone of a man on the verge of anger, stared a moment at this and then, in his natural voice, rejoined good-humoredly, "Upon my soul, I don't understand you!"

The change of key seemed to disconcert Glennard. "It's simple enough," he muttered.

"Simple enough—your offering me money in return for a friendly service? I don't know what your other friends expect!"

"Some of my friends wouldn't have undertaken the job. Those who would have done so would probably have expected to be paid."

He lifted his eyes to Flamel and the two men looked at each other. Flamel had turned white and his lips stirred, but he held his temperate note. "If you mean to imply that the job was not a nice one you lay yourself open to the retort that you proposed it. But for my part I've never seen, I never shall see, any reason for not publishing the letters."

"That's just it!"

"What—?"

"The certainty of your not seeing was what made me go to you. When a man's got stolen goods to pawn he doesn't take them to the police-station."

"Stolen?" Flamel echoed. "The letters were stolen?"

Glennard burst into a laugh. "How much longer do you expect me to keep up that pretence about the letters?

You knew well enough they were written to me."

Flamel looked at him in silence. "Were they?" he said at length. "I didn't know it."

"And didn't suspect it, I suppose," Glennard sneered.

The other was again silent; then he said, "I may remind you that, supposing I had felt any curiosity about the matter, I had no way of finding out that the letters were written to you. You never showed me the originals."

"What does that prove? There were fifty ways of finding out. It's the kind of thing one can easily do."

Flamel glanced at him with contempt. "Our ideas probably differ as to what a man can easily do. It would not have been easy for me."

Glennard's anger vented itself in the words uppermost in his thought. "It may, then, interest you to hear that my wife *does* know about the letters—has known for some months . . ."

"Ah," said the other, slowly.

Glennard saw that, in his blind clutch at a weapon, he had seized the one most apt to wound. Flamel's muscles were under control, but his face showed the undefinable change produced by the slow infiltration of poison. Every implication that the words contained had reached its mark; but Glennard felt that their obvious intent was lost in the anguish of what they suggested. He was sure now that Flamel would never have betrayed him; but the inference only made a wider outlet for his anger. He paused breathlessly for Flamel to speak.

"If she knows, it's not through me." It was what Glennard had waited for.

"Through you, by God? Who said it was through you? Do you suppose I leave it to you, or to anybody else, for that matter, to keep my wife informed of my actions? I didn't suppose even such egregious conceit as yours could delude a man to that degree!" Struggling for a foothold in the landslide of his dignity, he added in a steadier tone, "My wife learned the facts from me."

Flamel received this in silence. The other's outbreak seemed to have restored his self-control, and when he spoke it was with a deliberation implying that his course was chosen. "In that case I understand still less—"

"Still less—?"

"The meaning of this." He pointed to the check. "When you began to speak I supposed you had meant it as a bribe; now I can only infer it was intended as a random insult. In either case, here's my answer."

He tore the slip of paper in two and tossed the fragments across the desk to Glennard. Then he turned and walked out of the office.

Glennard dropped his head on his hands. If he had hoped to restore his self-respect by the simple expedient of assailing Flamel's, the result had not justified his expectation. The blow he had struck had blunted the edge of his anger, and the unforeseen extent of the hurt inflicted did not alter the fact that his weapon had broken in his hands. He now saw that his rage against Flamel was only the last projection of a passionate self-disgust. This consciousness did not dull his dislike of the man; it simply made reprisals ineffectual. Flamel's unwillingness to quarrel with him was the last stage of his abasement.

In the light of this final humiliation his assumption of his wife's indifference struck him as hardly so fatuous as the sentimental resuscitation of his past. He had been living in a factitious world wherein his emotions were the sycophants of his vanity, and it was with instinctive relief that he felt its ruins crash about his head.

It was nearly dark when he left his office, and he walked slowly homeward in the complete mental abeyance that follows on such a crisis. He was not aware that he was thinking of his wife; yet when he reached his own door he found that, in the involuntary readjustment of his vision, she had once more become the central point of consciousness.

13

*I*t had never before occurred to him that she might, after all, have missed the purport of the document he had put in her way. What if, in her hurried inspection of the papers, she had passed it over as related to the private business of some client? What, for instance, was to prevent her concluding that Glennard was the counsel of the unknown person who had sold the *Aubyn Letters?* The subject was one not likely to fix her attention—she was not a curious woman.

Glennard at this point laid down his fork and glanced at her between the candle-shades. The alternative explanation of her indifference was not slow in presenting itself. Her head had the same listening droop as when he had caught sight of her the day before in Flamel's company; the attitude revived the vividness of his impression. It was simple enough, after all. She had ceased to care for him because she cared for someone else.

As he followed her upstairs he felt a sudden stirring of his dormant anger. His sentiments had lost their artificial complexity. He had already acquitted her of any connivance in his baseness, and he felt only that he loved her and that she had escaped him. This was now, strangely enough, his dominant thought: the sense that he and she had passed through the fusion of love and had emerged from it as incommunicably apart as though the transmutation had never taken place. Every other passion, he mused, left some mark upon the nature; but love passed like the flight of a ship across the waters.

She dropped into her usual seat near the lamp, and he leaned against the chimney, moving about with an inattentive hand the knick-knacks on the mantel.

Suddenly he caught sight of her reflection in the mirror. She was looking at him. He turned and their eyes met.

He moved across the room.

"There's something that I want to say to you," he began.

She held his gaze, but her color deepened. He noticed again, with a jealous pang, how her beauty had gained in warmth and meaning. It was as though a transparent cup had been filled with wine. He looked at her ironically.

"I've never prevented your seeing your friends here," he broke out. "Why do you meet Flamel in out-of-the-way places? Nothing makes a woman so cheap—"

She rose abruptly and they faced each other a few feet apart.

"What do you mean?" she asked.

"I saw you with him last Sunday on the Riverside Drive," he went on, the utterance of the charge reviving his anger.

"Ah," she murmured. She sank into her chair again and began to play with a paper-knife that lay on the table at her elbow.

Her silence exasperated him.

"Well?" he burst out. "Is that all you have to say?"

"Do you wish me to explain?" she asked proudly.

"Do you imply I haven't the right to?"

"I imply nothing. I will tell you whatever you wish to know. I went for a walk with Mr. Flamel because he asked me to."

"I didn't suppose you went uninvited. But there are certain things a sensible woman doesn't do. She doesn't slink about in out-of-the-way streets with men. Why couldn't you have seen him here?"

She hesitated. "Because he wanted to see me alone."

"Did he indeed? And may I ask if you gratify all his wishes with equal alacrity?"

"I don't know that he has any others where I am concerned." She paused again and then continued, in a voice that somehow had an under-note of warning, "He wished to bid me good-bye. He's going away."

Glennard turned on her a startled glance. "Going away?"

"He's going to Europe to-morrow. He goes for a long time. I supposed you knew."

The last phrase revived his irritation. "You forget that I depend on you for my information about Flamel. He's your friend and not mine. In fact, I've sometimes wondered at your going out of your way to be so civil to him when you must see plainly enough that I don't like him."

Her answer to this was not immediate. She seemed to be choosing her words with care, not so much for her own sake as for his, and his exasperation was increased by the suspicion that she was trying to spare him.

"He was your friend before he was mine. I never knew him till I was married. It was you who brought him to the house and who seemed to wish me to like him."

Glennard gave a short laugh. The defence was feebler than he had expected: she was certainly not a clever woman.

"Your deference to my wishes is really beautiful; but it's not the first time in history that a man has made a mistake in introducing his friends to his wife. You must, at any rate, have seen since then that my enthusiasm had cooled; but so, perhaps, has your eagerness to oblige me."

She met this with a silence that seemed to rob the taunt of half its efficacy.

"Is that what you imply?" he pressed her.

"No," she answered with sudden directness. "I noticed some time ago that you seemed to dislike him, but since then—"

"Well—since then?"

"I've imagined that you had reasons for still wishing me to be civil to him, as you call it."

"Ah," said Glennard with an effort at lightness; but his irony dropped, for something in her voice made him feel that he and she stood at last in that naked desert of apprehension where meaning skulks vainly behind speech.

"And why did you imagine this?" The blood mounted to his forehead. "Because he told you that I was under obligations to him?"

She turned pale. "Under obligations?"

"Oh, don't let's beat about the bush. Didn't he tell you it was I who published Mrs. Aubyn's letters? Answer me that."

"No," she said; and after a moment which seemed given to the weighing of alternatives, she added: "No one told me."

"You didn't know, then?"

She seemed to speak with an effort. "Not until—not until—"

"Till I gave you those papers to sort?"

Her head sank.

"You understood then?"

"Yes."

He looked at her immovable face. "Had you suspected—before?" was slowly wrung from him.

"At times—yes—." Her voice dropped to a whisper.

"Why? From anything that was said—?"

There was a shade of pity in her glance. "No one said anything—no one told me anything." She looked away from him. "It was your manner—"

"My manner?"

"Whenever the book was mentioned. Things you said—once or twice—your irritation—I can't explain."

Glennard, unconsciously, had moved nearer. He breathed like a man who has been running. "You knew, then, you knew—" he stammered. The avowal of her love for Flamel would have hurt him less, would have rendered her less remote. "You knew—you knew—" he repeated; and suddenly his anguish gathered voice. "My God!" he cried, "you suspected it first, you say—and then you knew it—this damnable, this accursed thing; you knew it months ago—it's months since I put that paper in your way—and yet you've done nothing, you've said nothing, you've made no sign, you've lived alongside of me as if it had made no difference—no difference in either of our lives. What are you made of, I wonder? Don't you see the hideous ignominy of it? Don't you see how you've shared in my disgrace? Or haven't you any sense of shame?"

He preserved sufficient lucidity, as the words poured from him, to see how fatally they invited her derision; but something told him they had both passed beyond the phase of obvious retaliations, and that if any chord in her responded it would not be that of scorn.

He was right. She rose slowly and moved toward him.

"Haven't you had enough—without that?" she said in a strange voice of pity.

He stared at her. "Enough—?"

"Of misery . . ."

An iron band seemed loosened from his temples. "You saw then . . ?" he whispered.

"Oh, God—oh, God—" she sobbed. She dropped

beside him and hid her anguish against his knees. They clung thus in silence a long time, driven together down the same fierce blast of shame.

When at length she lifted her face he averted his. Her scorn would have hurt him less than the tears on his hands.

She spoke languidly, like a child emerging from a passion of weeping. "It was for the money—?"

His lips shaped an assent.

"That was the inheritance—that we married on?"

"Yes."

She drew back and rose to her feet. He sat watching her as she wandered away from him.

"You hate me," broke from him.

She made no answer.

"Say you hate me!" he persisted.

"That would have been so simple," she answered with a strange smile. She dropped into a chair near the writing-table and rested a bowed forehead on her hand.

"Was it much—?" she began at length.

"Much—?" he returned vaguely.

"The money."

"The money?" That part of it seemed to count so little that for a moment he did not follow her thought.

"It must be paid back," she insisted. "Can you do it?"

"Oh, yes," he returned listlessly. "I can do it."

"I would make any sacrifice for that!" she urged.

He nodded. "Of course." He sat staring at her in dry-eyed self-contempt. "Do you count on its making much difference?"

"Much difference?"

"In the way I feel—or you feel about me?"

She shook her head.

"It's the least part of it," he groaned.

"It's the only part we can repair."

"Good heavens! If there were any reparation—" He rose quickly and crossed the space that divided them. "Why did you never speak?"

"Haven't you answered that yourself?"

"Answered it?"

"Just now—when you told me you did it for me."

She paused a moment and then went on with a deepening note—"I would have spoken if I could have helped you."

"But you must have despised me."

"I've told you that would have been simpler."

"But how could you go on like this—hating the money?"

"I knew you'd speak in time. I wanted you, first, to hate it as I did."

He gazed at her with a kind of awe. "You're wonderful," he murmured. "But you don't yet know the depths I've reached."

She raised an entreating hand. "I don't want to!"

"You're afraid, then, that you'll hate me?"

"No—but that you'll hate *me.* Let me understand without your telling me."

"You can't. It's too base. I thought you didn't care because you loved Flamel."

She blushed deeply. "Don't—don't—" she warned him.

"I haven't the right to, you mean?"

"I mean that you'll be sorry."

He stood imploringly before her. "I want to say something worse—something more outrageous. If you don't understand *this* you'll be perfectly justified in ordering me out of the house."

She answered him with a glance of divination. "I shall understand—but you'll be sorry."

"I must take my chance of that." He moved away and tossed the books about the table. Then he swung round and faced her. "Does Flamel care for you?" he asked.

Her flush deepened, but she still looked at him without anger. "What would be the use?" she said with a note of sadness.

"Ah, I didn't ask *that*," he penitently murmured.

"Well, then—"

To this adjuration he made no response beyond that of gazing at her with an eye which seemed now to view her as a mere factor in an immense redistribution of meanings.

"I insulted Flamel to-day. I let him see that I suspected him of having told you. I hated him because he knew about the letters."

He caught the spreading horror of her eyes, and for an instant he had to grapple with the new temptation they lit up. Then he said with an effort—"Don't blame him—he's impeccable. He helped me to get them published; but I lied to him too; I pretended they were written to another man . . . a man who was dead . . ."

She raised her arms in a gesture that seemed to ward off his blows.

"You *do* despise me!" he insisted.

"Ah, that poor woman—that poor woman—" he heard her murmur.

"I spare no one, you see!" he triumphed over her. She kept her face hidden.

"You do hate me, you do despise me!" he strangely exulted.

"Be silent!" she commanded him; but he seemed no longer conscious of any check on his gathering purpose.

"He cared for you—he cared for you," he repeated, "and he never told you of the letters—"

She sprang to her feet. "How can you?" she flamed. "How dare you? *That—!*"

Glennard was ashy pale. "It's a weapon . . . like another . . ."

"A scoundrel's!"

He smiled wretchedly. "I should have used it in his place."

"Stephen! Stephen!" she cried, as though to drown the blasphemy on his lips. She swept to him with a rescuing gesture. "Don't say such things. I forbid you! It degrades us both."

He put her back with trembling hands. "Nothing that I say of myself can degrade you. We're on different levels."

"I'm on yours, wherever it is!"

He lifted his head and their gaze flowed together.

14

The great renewals take effect as imperceptibly as the first workings of spring. Glennard, though he felt himself brought nearer to his wife, was still, as it were, hardly within speaking distance. He was but laboriously acquiring the rudiments of a new language; and he had to grope for her through the dense fog of his humiliation, the distorting vapor against which his personality loomed grotesque and mean.

Only the fact that we are unaware how well our nearest know us enables us to live with them. Love is the most impregnable refuge of self-esteem, and we hate the eye that reaches to our nakedness. If Glennard did not hate his wife it was slowly, sufferingly, that there was born in him that profounder passion which made his earlier feeling seem a mere commotion of the blood. He was like a child coming back to the sense of an enveloping presence: her nearness was a breast on which he leaned.

They did not, at first, talk much together, and each beat a devious track about the outskirts of the subject that lay between them like a haunted wood. But every word, every action, seemed to glance at it, to draw toward it, as though a fount of healing sprang in its poisoned shade. If only they might cut a way through the thicket to that restoring spring!

Glennard, watching his wife with the intentness of a wanderer to whom no natural sign is negligeable, saw that she had taken temporary refuge in the purpose of renouncing the money. If both, theoretically, owned the inefficacy of such amends, the woman's instinctive subjectiveness made her find relief in this crude form of penance. Glennard saw that she meant to live as frugally as possible till what she deemed their debt was discharged; and he prayed she might not discover how far-reaching, in its merely material sense, was the obligation she thus hoped to acquit. Her mind was fixed on the sum originally paid for the letters, and this he knew he could lay aside in a year or two. He was touched, meanwhile, by the spirit that made her discard the petty luxuries which she regarded as the sign of their bondage. Their shared renunciations drew her nearer to him, helped, in their evidence of her helplessness, to restore the full protecting stature of his love. And still they did not speak.

It was several weeks later that, one afternoon by the drawing-room fire, she handed him a letter that she had been reading when he entered.

"I've heard from Mr. Flamel," she said.

It was as though a latent presence had become visible to both. Glennard took the letter mechanically.

"It's from Smyrna," she said. "Won't you read it?"

He handed it back. "You can tell me about it—his hand's so illegible." He wandered to the other end of the room and then turned and stood before her. "I've been thinking of writing to Flamel," he said.

She looked up.

"There's one point," he continued slowly, "that I ought to clear up. I told him you'd known about the letters all along; for a long time, at least; and I saw how it hurt him. It was just what I meant to do, of course; but I can't leave him to that false impression; I must write him."

She received this without outward movement, but he saw that the depths were stirred. At length she returned in a hesitating tone, "Why do you call it a false impression? I did know."

"Yes, but I implied you didn't care."

"Ah!"

He still stood looking down on her. "Don't you want me to set that right?" he pursued.

She lifted her head and fixed him bravely. "It isn't necessary," she said.

Glennard flushed with the shock of the retort; then, with a gesture of comprehension, "No," he said, "with you it couldn't be; but I might still set myself right."

She looked at him gently. "Don't I," she murmured, "do that?"

"In being yourself merely? Alas, the rehabilitation's too complete! You make me seem—to myself even— what I'm not; what I can never be. I can't, at times, defend myself from the delusion; but I can at least enlighten others."

The flood was loosened, and kneeling by her he caught her hands. "Don't you see that it's become an obsession with me? That if I could strip myself down to the last lie—only there'd always be another one left under it!—and do penance naked in the market-place, I should at least have the relief of easing one anguish by another? Don't you see that the worst of my torture is the impossibility of such amends?"

Her hands lay in his without returning pressure. "Ah, poor woman, poor woman," he heard her sigh.

"Don't pity her, pity me! What have I done to her or to you, after all? You're both inaccessible! It was myself I sold."

He took an abrupt turn away from her; then halted before her again. "How much longer," he burst out, "do you suppose you can stand it? You've been magnificent, you've been inspired, but what's the use? You can't wipe out the ignominy of it. It's miserable for you and it does *her* no good!"

She lifted a vivid face. "That's the thought I can't bear!" she cried.

"What thought?"

"That it does her no good—all you're feeling, all you're suffering. Can it be that it makes no difference?"

He avoided her challenging glance. "What's done is done," he muttered.

"Is it ever, quite, I wonder?" she mused. He made no answer and they lapsed into one of the pauses that are a subterranean channel of communication.

It was she who, after a while, began to speak, with a new suffusing diffidence that made him turn a roused eye on her.

"Don't they say," she asked, feeling her way as in a kind of tender apprehensiveness, "that the early Christians, instead of pulling down the heathen temples—the temples of the unclean gods—purified them by turning them to their own uses? I've always thought one might do that with one's actions—the actions one loathes but can't undo. One can make, I mean, a wrong the door to other wrongs or an impassable wall against them . . ." Her voice wavered on the word. "We can't always tear down the temples we've built to the unclean gods, but we can put good spirits in the house of evil—the spirits of mercy and shame and understanding, that might never have come to us if we hadn't been in such great need . . ."

She moved over to him and laid a hand on his. His head was bent and he did not change his attitude. She sat down beside him without speaking; but their silences now were fertile as rain-clouds—they quickened the seeds of understanding.

At length he looked up. "I don't know," he said, "what spirits have come to live in the house of evil that I built—but you're there and that's enough. It's strange," he went on after another pause, "she wished the best for me so often, and now, at last, it's through her that it's come to me. But for her I shouldn't have known you—it's through her that I've found you. Sometimes—do you know?—that makes it hardest—makes me most intolerable to myself. Can't you see that it's the worst thing I've got to face? I sometimes think I could have borne it better if you hadn't understood! I took everything from her—everything—even to the poor shelter of loyalty she'd trusted in—the only thing I *could* have left her!—I took everything from her, I deceived her, I despoiled her, I destroyed her—and she's given me *you* in return!"

His wife's cry caught him up. "It isn't that she's given *me* to you—it is that she's given you to yourself." She leaned to him as though swept forward on a wave of pity. "Don't you see," she went on, as his eyes hung on her, "that that's the gift you can't escape from, the debt you're pledged to acquit? Don't you see that you've never before been what she thought you, and that now, so wonderfully, she's made you into the man she loved? *That's* worth suffering for, worth dying for, to a woman—that's the gift she would have wished to give!"

"Ah," he cried, "but woe to him by whom it cometh. What did I ever give her?"

"The happiness of giving," she said.

BY EDITH WHARTON

THE GREATER INCLINATION

12mo $1.50

CONTENTS

OPINIONS OF THE PRESS

¶

Eight pieces of delicate texture and artistic conception. Every
one of them has the external shape and coloring of the world in
which we mingle day by day, and every one of them is at heart
a poignant spiritual tragedy. This may sound like extravagant
praise, but no conventional commendation would be adequate
for such a book. Between these stories and those of the ordinary entertaining sort there is a great gulf fixed. — *The Dial*.

¶

Marked by great technical skill, by keen humor, and by a style
which is individual and striking. There is a quality of distinction
about her work not merely of style but of character. — *The New
York Sun*.

¶

This book of short stories comes out of America, and it is good.
It is very good. Mrs. Wharton is one of the few to grasp that obvious but much neglected fact that the first business of a writer
is to be able to write. "The Greater Inclination" is distinguished
and delightful. — *The Academy*.

¶

If we were to single out one book from those that have been
published this season as exhibiting in the highest degree that

rare creative power called literary genius, we should name "The Greater Inclination," by Mrs. Edith Wharton. — *The Bookman*.

¶

Her style is as finished as a cameo, and there is nowhere an indication of haste or crudity or the least inattention to detail. Only a woman to the manner born in society, a woman, too, whose literary favorites or her literary masters may have been Thackeray or James, since she partakes of the spirit of the one, and has followed the exquisite workmanship of the other, could have written "The Pelican" or "Souls Belated." — *Literature*.

¶

Mrs. Wharton has not only observed people carefully, but has really perceived the subtle significance of their ordinary aspects, so that her figures are not only individuals but types. This sympathetic and suggestive portrayal and the generally optimistic and moral tone make "The Greater Inclination" a book of really great value. — *Boston Transcript*.

¶

Mrs. Wharton shows us so much delicacy of touch, so much clarity and neatness of style, and at times so much profundity of comprehension as to make her volume quite unique among the books that have been sent to us this year. . . . We could go on quoting indefinitely, so full is Mrs. Wharton's book of thoughts that are startlingly original in substance and given with a most vivid sense of form ; but we prefer to commend the volume most unreservedly to every reader, since nothing that we have seen this year in fiction-writing has seemed to us so memorable, both in its choice of subjects, its mastery of style, and its piquant art that makes one think and wonder. — *N. Y. Commercial Advertiser*.

CHARLES SCRIBNER'S SONS, PUBLISHERS
153–157 FIFTH AVENUE, NEW YORK

Epilogue

*L*ike many successful women, Edith Wharton usually sought to conceal the difficulty and occasional despair that beset her. Thus although *The Touchstone* is suggestive, it is far from confessional, and some of the novel's weaknesses (an ending that seems inconclusive, for instance) may be the result of her desire to eliminate all traces of "self" from the novel.

Nonetheless, a perceptive reader can make several inferences from this narrative. For example, one might conclude that Wharton's decision to focus on Glennard's shallowness was a powerful if indirect revelation of her own concerns—that his smugly condescending image of the "poor woman of genius . . . [living in] her cold niche of fame" and his assumption that if Margaret Aubyn "had been prettier she would have had emotions instead of ideas" reiterated stereotypes the novelist had encountered all too often herself. These are forms of the notion that a "true woman" will seek not to create beauty but to be beautiful. Another reflection of the same ideology lies behind Glennard's fatuous conviction that because she looked like "a throned Justice," the entire range of Alexa Trent's moral concern could be acknowledged merely by appreciating the beauty of her face.

Recent scholarship has suggested that the text of *The Touchstone* may even bear significant traces of the ridicule that Wharton had suffered in her youth. Anyone who has been subjected to repeated humiliation (typically, as the offspring of parents whose notions of "discipline" entail such treatment) will have internalized this behavior; and such a person will carry a deep and abiding sense of shame into adulthood. There are many ways for adults to manage the discomfort of this feeling; and they may even be so skillful at disguising it that virtually no one can recognize the pain they experience repeatedly. Nonetheless, the legacy of shame is a burden—always an agonizing burden, sometimes even a crippling one. And as many feminist scholars have recently observed, it is a burden borne by women in disproportionate numbers because women have so frequently been ridiculed for engaging in behavior that is judged perfectly normal or entirely acceptable in men. Indeed, it may even be the case that the intense anger that can be found in some female *Künstlerromane* expresses not merely the appropriate adult outrage at the limitations that have been imposed upon women, but also a residue of anger at the many, many episodes of belittlement that creative women have been subjected to until very recently (since such females could develop their talent only by doing things defined as "inappropriate for girls"). Certainly much of Wharton's work bears the traces of just such an experience.

In *Edith Wharton's Prisoners of Shame,* Lev Raphael begins by describing the evidence that permits us to infer that some past pattern of humiliation and ridicule has been internalized as shame: "In a general sense, internalized shame is 'experienced as a deep abiding sense of being defective. . . .' This central affect-belief gradually recedes from consciousness and becomes the unconscious core of the personality. We no longer have to suffer real defeats, rejections or failure; just *perceiving* events in these ways or even *anticipating* failure can confirm our sense of shame." Raphael then proceeds to examine Wharton's first novel, revealing it to be almost a case-study of this phenomenon:

> . . . It is hard to miss the prevalence of shame in *The Touchstone.* At the linguistic level, the words "shame," "ashamed," "humiliation," "humiliated" and various synonyms like "abasement," "dishonor," and "baseness" appear with insistent frequency, sometimes twice in a paragraph. But more importantly, the felt experience of shame is communicated with depth and brilliance from the very beginning of the novella.

In the real world, it was, of course, the future novelist Edith Wharton who had experienced the unrelenting process that had produced shame. Any sensitive reader might suppose that, like her creator, Mrs. Aubyn was susceptible to this insidious emotion. However, *The Touchstone* tells us virtually nothing about Mrs. Aubyn's feelings, and in this novel, it is primarily Glennard who bears the burden of shame.

This is an interesting displacement. No one within the novel ridicules Glennard. Yet his insensitivity in dealing with Margaret Aubyn and his callousness in marketing their intimate correspondence will move most readers to an unvoiced but nonetheless powerful revulsion. Thus his enactment of shame seems only "appropriate" to most readers, the response Glennard "must be feeling" to what so many of the people he meets "would think" if only they knew the truth. In Wharton's female *Künstlerroman,* then, the tables have been turned: it is not the "scribbling woman" who must suffer ridicule, but rather the man who both rejects her and attempts to exploit her.

Here again, however, Edith Wharton's personal relationship to the novel is indirect at best: we can infer that an author who is so preoccupied with the nuances of shame and who so often includes them in her work may have had the personal experience of suffering from unkind, belittling criticism; however, the novel itself offers few clues to the exact nature of this ridicule, and only Edith Wharton's letters and private notebooks can give substance to this intuition.

In one respect, however, *The Touchstone* was intensely, inescapably personal. Having declined to reveal its author's past, it nonetheless foretold her future. It is a true *Künstlerroman,* but in reverse: it is directly revelatory about the author's life, not as it had been but as it would be. Even the general reading public could see a small part of this prophetic element: like Margaret Aubyn, Edith Wharton went to live permanently in Europe, where women of intelligence and accomplishment were not generally regarded as freaks of nature. However, until very recently, the most astonishingly prophetic elements in this novel were known to no more than three or four people.

Edith Wharton had married her husband, Teddy, in 1885. Never an ecstatic relationship nor one of intellectual intimacy, the marriage was companionable enough for many years. Nonetheless, there were no children to reinforce the relationship, and after a while, the couple grew apart. By 1905, when Edith Wharton's first bestseller, *The House of Mirth,* assured her international fame, Teddy had grown resentful, and his resentfulness was made more problematic by severe mood swings—from dizzying elation to profound dejection. In 1907, Edith Wharton met a journalist named Morton Fullerton, who soon became her lover; and in 1913 Edith and Teddy Wharton were divorced. This was Wharton's only affair, an exhilarating sexual awakening and for many years a genuinely deep commitment. Yet even after her divorce, Wharton did not want to marry Fullerton, and after six or seven years, the relationship ended quietly.

During Wharton's lifetime, the divorce was only part of this scenario that was known to other people. Although many of Wharton's friends were acquainted with Morton Fullerton, only one or two suspected the intimacy; and after her death in 1937, the connection to Fullerton, even the record of their friendship, dropped into almost complete obscurity. The reading public did not learn about the affair until the mid-1970s, and by then few facts about Fullerton's life had been preserved. It is true that the lovers were often separated and that when they were, Wharton had written a good many letters; yet she had destroyed Fullerton's letters to her, and she had requested that he do the same with her letters. Since none of the correspondence came to light, it was assumed that Fullerton had complied with her wish. Thus scholars were taken by complete surprise when a European bookseller surfaced in the early 1980s and announced that he was in possession of Wharton's letters to Morton Fullerton—more than three hundred of them.

In 1988, an edition of Wharton's letters was published, containing a generous sample of the elusive correspondence. And so the veil of privacy and reticence that she had so artfully drawn during her lifetime was finally pulled aside. One result was that the full extent of unconscious self-revelation in *The Touchstone* could finally be seen.

Morton Fullerton turns out to have been a man very much like Glennard: although he was more sophisticated and experienced, he had the same weakness of character—not malicious so much as insufficiently fastidious. He did not deliberately set out to prey upon Edith Wharton's affections for "what he could get out of her"; nevertheless, he pursued her until he had won her affections, and then he dallied with them for several years. It may have pleased his vanity to have power over this woman, whose intelligence and talent were patently greater than his own and whose emotions were both deeper and more complex. In any case, even though Edith Wharton eventually requested either that he return her letters or destroy them— in short, made every effort to keep the intimacies of the relationship entirely private, Fullerton ignored all her pleas. The only aspect of their relationship about which he was meticulous was this one: he saved all of Edith Wharton's letters, and eventually (after her death), he sold them.

They disclose the great woman novelist in an almost embarrassingly humbled attitude, for Fullerton was a far from faithful lover. For his part, Morton Fullerton was more than willing to trade upon Wharton's literary prominence: she loaned him money (which he never repaid); she sent work his way when she had the opportunity to do so. And he used her affection without troubling to feel any emotional obligation to her. At first, Whartonians may feel discomfited by the relationship—so much openness and generosity on her part, such exploitation on his. Yet in the end, Fullerton seems not so much a villain as merely a petty thief. Thus our final assessment of these unexpected letters may best be framed by paraphrasing *The Touchstone:* Edith Wharton's correspondence is really a series of " '*unloved* letters' . . . 'A man who could let [this distinguished woman] write to him in that way? . . . I pity him.'"

We cannot even transform these events into melodrama or tragedy. If Morton Fullerton was like Glennard—obtuse in the presence of genius—Edith Wharton was not unlike Margaret Aubyn. She gained much from the liaison. She lost much, too. Yet this was not an undying love, and she was not devastated by his perfidy. Confronted by the inescapable flaws of his nature, she eventually chose simply to withdraw. Nor should we even be disappointed by this distinguished woman's "weakness"—several years of an unsuccessful affair of the heart.

Edith Wharton had been born into an era when all "normal" women were supposed to be passive, inarticulate, and utterly devoid of passion. Her family, for whatever reasons, elected to "punish" her refusals to conform to this norm by depriving her of the opportunity to write and by ridiculing her unmercifully. Despite these obstacles, despite the conflict that sometimes threatened to immobilize her, Edith Wharton claimed her right to emotional maturity—as a woman and as a writer—and she used her fiction to excoriate the ways in which all women were disadvantaged by their culture. Early in her life, she discovered that work was the best tonic for health, and there is no doubt that the pursuit of her career enhanced her self-esteem and vigor. Nor was its value limited to her own life. Wharton has imparted strength to many generations of readers by giving them the emotional insight and the encouragement to alter society's debilitating norms. That combination of achievements is a considerable triumph. If her adult life had been so cautiously limited that she permitted herself no mistakes of the heart, that fact would be considerably more disappointing than the details of this imprudent liaison.

The "prophetic" mission of *The Touchstone* was finally completed in 1913 or 1914 (not long after her divorce) when the love affair with Fullerton was over. Edith Wharton's work continued with ever-increasing power, reinvigorated by her freedom from the unhappy emotional entanglements of both the painful marriage and the frustrating affair, and she went on to become America's most accomplished woman novelist—happy and finally at peace. Morton Fullerton slipped quietly into obscurity. Almost a century later, he would enjoy modest celebrity when a number of scholars learned to recognize his name (though not to admire him). He was fated to be known for only one thing: he was the man who had marketed his love-letters from Edith Wharton.

Selected Bibliography

Baym, Nina. *Women's Fiction: A Guide to Novels By and About Women in America, 1820–1870.* Ithaca and London: Cornell University Press, 1978.

Belenky, Mary Field, Blythe McVicker Clinchy, Nancy Rule Goldberger, and Jill Mattuck Tarule. *Women's Ways of Knowing: The Development of Self, Voice, and Mind.* New York: Basic Books, 1986.

Douglas, Ann. *The Feminization of American Culture.* New York: Alfred A. Knopf, 1977.

———— [published under the name Ann D. Wood]. "The 'Scribbling Women' and Fanny Fern: Why Women Wrote," in *American Quarterly* XXIII (Spring 1971), no. 1, 3–25.

Fern, Fanny. *Ruth Hall,* Joyce W. Warren, ed. New Brunswick and London: Rutgers University Press, 1988.

Gilligan, Carol. *In a Different Voice.* Cambridge, Massachusetts and London: Harvard University Press, 1982.

Huf, Linda. *A Portrait of the Artist as a Young Woman: The Writer as Heroine in American Literature.* New York: Frederick Ungar Publishing Co., 1984.

Kaufman, Gershen. *Shame.* Cambridge, Massachusetts: Schenkman Publishing Co., Inc., 1985.

Lewis, R.W.B. *Edith Wharton.* New York: Harper & Row, 1975.

Lynd, H.M. *On Shame and the Search for Identity.* New York: Harcourt Brace, 1958.

Moers, Ellen. *Literary Women: The Great Writers.* New York: Doubleday & Co., 1977.

Olsen, Tillie. *Silences.* New York: Delacorte Press/Seymour Lawrence, 1978.

Phelps, Elizabeth Stuart. *The Story of Avis,* Carol Farley Kessler, ed. New Brunswick and London: Rutgers University Press, 1985.

Raphael, Lev. *Edith Wharton's Prisoners of Shame.* New York: St. Martin's Press [in press].

Russ, Joanna. *How to Suppress Women's Writing.* Austin: University of Texas Press, 1983.

Sanford, Linda Tschirhart, and Mary Ellen Donovan. *Women and Self-Esteem.* New York: Penguin Books, 1985.

Spacks, Patricia Meyer. "Selves in Hiding," in *Women's Autobiography: Essays in Criticism*, Estelle G. Jelinek, ed. Bloomington: Indiana University Press, 1980.

Tompkins, Jane. *Sensational Designs: The Cultural Work of American Fiction, 1790–1860.* Oxford, New York, and Toronto: Oxford University Press, 1985.

Wharton, Edith. *A Backward Glance* and "Life and I," in *Novellas and Other Writings,* Cynthia Griffin Wolff, ed. New York: Literary Classics of the United States, Inc., 1990.

———. *The Letters of Edith Wharton,* R.W.B. Lewis and Nancy Lewis, eds. New York: Charles Scribner's Sons, 1988.

Wolff, Cynthia Griffin. *A Feast of Words: The Triumph of Edith Wharton.* New York and Oxford: Oxford University Press, 1977.